BIGGLES, PIONEER AIR FIGHTER

Other books by Captain W. E. Johns in Armada

BIGGLES

PIONEER AIR FIGHTER

Captain W. E. Johns

Armada

First published in the U.K. in 1932 under the title
The Camels are Coming by John Hamilton Ltd., London.
First published as *Biggles, Pioneer Air Fighter*
in 1954 by Thames Publishing Co., London.
This edition was first published in Armada in 1982 by
Fontana Paperbacks, 14 St James's Place,
London SW1A 1PS.

© W. E. Johns (Publications) Ltd.

Printed in Great Britain by
Love & Malcomson Ltd., Brighton Road,
Redhill, Surrey.

CONTENTS

ABOUT PIONEER AIR COMBAT

by Captain W. E. Johns

CAPTAIN JAMES BIGGLESWORTH is a fictitious character, yet he could have been found in any R.F.C. mess during those great days of 1917 and 1918 when air combat had become the order of the day and air duelling was a fine art.

To readers who are unfamiliar with the conditions that prevailed in the sky of France during the last two years of World War I, it may seem unlikely that so many adventures could have fallen to the lot of one man. In these eventful years, every day—and I might almost say every hour—brought adventure, tragic or humorous, to the man in the air, and as we sat in our cockpits warming up our engines for the dawn "show", no one could say what the end of the day would bring, or whether he would be alive to see it.

Again, it may seem improbable that any one man could have been involved in so many hazardous undertakings, and yet survive. That may be true; sooner or later most war pilots met the inevitable fate of the flying fighter. I sometimes wonder how any of us survived, yet there were some who seemed to bear a charmed life. William Bishop, the British ace, Rene Fonck, the French ace and prince of air duellists, and, on the other side, Ernest Udet, and many others, fought hundreds of battles in the air and survived thousands of hours of deadly peril. Every day incredible deeds of heroism were performed by pilots whose names are unknown.

Nowhere are the curious whims of Lady Luck so apparent as in the air. Lothar von Richthofen, brother of the famous ace, shot down forty British machines and was killed in a simple cross-country flight. Nungesser, the French champion of forty-five air battles, was drowned, and McKeever, Canadian ace of thirty victories, was killed in a skidding motor-car. Captain "Jock" McKay, of my squadron, survived three years' air warfare only to be killed by "archie" an hour before the Armistice was signed. Lieutenant A. E. Amey, who fought his first and last fight beside me, had not even unpacked his kit! I have spun into the ground out of control yet lived to tell the tale. Gordon, of my squadron, made a good landing, but bumped on an old road that ran across the aerodrome, turned turtle, and broke his neck.

Again, should the sceptic think I have been guilty of exaggeration, I would say that exaggeration is almost impossible where air combat is concerned. The speed at which a dog-fight took place and the amazing manner in which machines appeared from nowhere, and could disappear, apparently into thin air, was so bewildering as to baffle description. It is beyond my ability to convey adequately the sensation of being one of ten or a dozen machines, zooming, whirling, and diving among the maze of pencil-lines that marked the track of tracer bullets. One could not exaggerate the horror of seeing two machines collide head-on a few yards away, and words have yet to be coined to express that tightening of the heart-strings that comes of seeing one of your own side roaring down in a sheet of flame. Seldom was any attempt made by spectators to describe these things at the time; they were best forgotten.

It is not surprising that many strange incidents occurred, incidents that were never written down on combat reports, but were whispered in dim corners of the hangars while we were waiting for the order to start up, for the "late birds" to come home to roost. It was "H", a tall South African S.E. pilot, who came in white-faced and told me he had just shot down a Camel by mistake. It was the Camel pilot's fault. He playfully zoomed over the S.E., apparently out of sheer light-heartedness. "H" told me that he started shooting when he saw the shadow; he turned and saw the red, white and blue circles, but it was too late. He had already gripped the Bowden control and fired a burst of not more than five rounds. He had fired hundreds of rounds at enemy aircraft without hitting one, but the Camel fell in flames. He asked me if he should report it, and I, rightly or wrongly, said no, for nothing could bring the Camel back. "H" went West soon afterwards.

Almost everybody has heard the story told by Boe-like, the German ace, of how he once found a British machine with a dead crew flying a ghostly course amid the clouds. On another occasion he shot down an F.E., which, spinning viciously, threw its observer out behind the German lines and the pilot behind the British lines. What of the R.E.8 that landed perfectly behind our lines with pilot and observer stiff and stark in their cockpits! The R.E.8 was not an easy machine to land at any time, as those who flew it will remember.

Rene Fonck once shot down a German machine which threw out its pilot; machine and man fell straight through a formation of Spads below without touching one of them! The German pilot was Wissemann, who had just shot down Guynemer, Fonck's friend and brother ace, but he did not know that at the time. The coincidence is worth noting. Madon, another ace, once attacked a German two-seater at point-blank range—his usual method. A bullet struck the goggles off the Boche observer and sent them whirling into the air; Madon caught them on his wires and brought them home. When Warneford shot down his Zeppelin, one of the crew jumped from the blazing airship, and after falling for a distance generally believed to be about 200 feet, crashed through the roof of a convent and landed on a bed that had just been vacated by a nun. He lived to tell the tale.

One could go on with such stories indefinitely, but these should be sufficient to show that, in the air at least, truth is stranger than fiction.

Many of the adventures that are ascribed to Biggles did actually occur, and are true in their essential facts. Students of air history may identify them. In some cases the officers concerned are still alive and serving in the Royal Air Force.

Finally, I hope that from a perusal of these pages a younger generation of air fighters may learn something of the tricks of the trade, of the traps and pitfalls that beset the unwary, for I fear that many of the lessons which we learned in the hard school of war are being rapidly obscured by the mists of peace-time theory. In air-fighting, one week of experience is worth a year of peace-time practice. In peace a man may make a mistake—and live. He may not even know of his mistake. If he makes that same mistake in war—he dies, unless it is his lucky day, in which case the error is so vividly brought to his notice that he is never guilty of it again.

No one can say just how he will react when, for the first time, he hears the slash of bullets ripping through his machine. The sound has turned boys into grey-faced men, and even hardened campaigners who learnt their business on the ground have felt their lips turn dry.

In the following pages certain expressions occur from time to time in connection with the tactics of air combat which may seem to the layman to be out of proportion to their importance. For instance, he will read of "getting into the sun". It is quite impossible for any-body who does not fly to realise what this means and how utterly impossible it is to see what is going on in that direction, particularly when the sun is low and one is flying west. To fly into the face of the setting sun can be uncomfortable at any time, but the strain of trying to peer into the glare, knowing that it may discharge a squadron of enemy aircraft at any moment, becomes torture after a time.

It should also be remembered that an aeroplane is an extremely small vehicle and difficult to see. When one is on the ground it is the noise of the engine that almost invariably first attracts attention, and but for the un-mistakeable telltale hum, few would be seen at all. In the air, the roar of one's own engine drowns all other sound, and one is therefore dependent upon sight alone for detecting the presence of other aircraft. This fact should be borne in mind when reading stories of the air, and particularly of air combat.

Constant reference is also made to "archie". Most people know by now that this was not an old friend whom we called by his Christian name. There was nothing friendly about archie. On the contrary, it often bit you when you were least expecting it, but on the whole its bark was worse than its bite. Archie was the war-pilot's nickname for anti-aircraft gun-fire. During the war, archie batteries stretched from the North Sea to the Swiss frontier; its appearance in the sky was accepted as a matter of course, and dodging it was part of the daily round. After a time one became accustomed to it and ignored it unless it was very bad.

HOW BIGGLES WAS "BORN"

THESE stories of World War I were written about a character whose exploits—little suspected by me at the time—were to continue to the present day. They were written for a magazine of which I was the editor, and apart from the entertainment of the reader, had the more serious purpose of presenting a picture of war flying as it was in its infancy. It seems unlikely that anyone could have suspected the developments that were to follow and astonish us in World War II.

In the 1914 war, flying began with pilots trying to drop stones on each other. The pistol followed, then the carbine, and the first casualties occurred. The next step was an ordinary ground machine-gun. Later, this was fixed to the machine. A great stride was made when a timing gear was produced to allow first one, then two, machine-guns to fire forward through the airscrew—at that time incorrectly called a propeller. Even in 1918 armament was still primitive compared with the types that fought in the Battle of Britain. Air combat was mostly a matter of "catch as catch can", with every man for himself. Tricks and ruses were common. Discipline was casual, for the senior officers of the R.F.C. had not had time to grow old.

In short, it was the era of experiment, of trial and error. But it was from the apparently irresponsible behaviour of the pilots of the Kaiser's war that the traditions of the air service emerged. Discipline, speed and striking power may have been stepped up, but the human factor is the same.

W.E.J.

GLOSSARY OF TERMS

Altimeter: The instrument used for determining the height of an aeroplane. It is not unlike a barometer, and is set in the instrument board.

Ammonal: A very powerful explosive. It was used in Mills bombs.

Archie: The old Royal Flying Corps expression for anti-aircraft gun-fire. In World War II it became "flak".

"Blipping": The art of opening the throttle of a rotary engine in short, sharp bursts to keep it "alive".

Bomb-Toggle: The bomb release handle.

Bowden Lever: The machine-guns of certain aeroplanes were fired by depressing a lever on the joystick. Sometimes a thumb button was used in the top of the joystick. Other methods were also employed according to the type of machine.

Brass-Hats: A common expression meaning staff officers, no doubt originating from the gold device on the peaks of their caps—often referred to as "bananas".

Bristol Fighter: A famous type of two-seater British all-purpose aeroplane.

Buckingham: A type of incendiary bullet, calculated to set fire to anything it hit. They were used chiefly against lighter-than-air craft in order to set fire to the hydrogen gas with which these were inflated.

Camouflage: A word coined from the French, meaning "to conceal", "disguise", or make a thing look like something it was not. Many different forms of camouflage were employed during the war. Imitation grass mats, spread above guns, was known as camouflage. The paintings of buildings, hangars and guns in sections of different colours, in order to break up their outlines, was also known as camouflage.

Centre Section: That part of the top plane of an aeroplane which comes immediately over the fuselage, and to which the wings themselves are joined.

Circus: Formations of enemy aeroplanes were commonly called circuses; often they were known by the name of the leader: thus "Richthofen's circus".

Cooper Bombs: Special bombs generally reckoned to weigh twenty pounds, although as a matter of fact they usually weighed about twenty-five pounds; often carried by single-seat fighters under the wings, four each side.

Deflection: The allowance made when shooting at a moving target. Briefly, it means shooting at the place where the target is expected to be when the missile reaches it.

Double-Frontiers: In order to prevent prisoners of war from escaping, the Germans, in many places, arranged artificial or false frontiers in order to lead escaping officers to believe that they had entered another country, whereas in fact they had not.

Fanning (Down): An R.F.C. expression for blowing up with bombs. Things were fanned down, not blown up.

Flaming Onions: Missiles used by the Germans against aeroplanes in World War I. The weapons that fired them remained a mystery until the end of the war. They appeared in a series of glowing balls of fire that rose vertically from the ground.

Flying Wire: Broadly speaking, the wings of biplanes were braced with two sorts of wires, flying wires and landing wires. Flying wires hold the wings in position in the air; landing wires take the weight of the wings when the machine is standing on the ground.

Hannoverana: An efficient type of German two-seater, 1917-18.

Inclinometer: An instrument very much like a spirit-level, set across the instrument board, the position of the bubble showing if the machine is flying level, or banking.

M.O.: Medical Officer.

"Nines": De Havilland 9s, famous 2-seater bombers, 1917-18.

Parachute Flares: Bright lights which had a parachute attachment in order that they should sink slowly to the ground. They were used by aeroplanes to illuminate the ground below them while night-flying.

Pour Vous: Words supposed to resemble the noise made by the German Mercédès aero engine.

Rocking Wings: The signal usually employed (before the days of radio) by the leader of a formation to indicate that enemy aircraft were in sight or that he was going to attack.

Rumpler: A German two-seater aeroplane used in large quantities during the war.

"Sausage": Kite balloons were sometimes called "sausages". German balloons were sometimes referred to as *Drachens*.

"Shoot" (Artillery): A machine spotting for the artillery was said to be doing a "shoot".

Sidcot (suit): A thick, padded overall garment worn by pilots.

Smudge Fire: A small fire usually kept alight on aerodromes to show landing machines the direction of the wind.

Spandaus: Many German machine-guns and bullets were made at Spandau, Germany. For this reason German machine-guns were often referred to as Spandaus.

Tarmac: The paved area in front of the hangars.

Triplane: An aeroplane having three wings is a triplane. During the war it usually meant the Fokker triplane;

also called "Tripehound". Sopwith triplanes were used by the British.

Very Pistol: A short, large-bore pistol used for firing signal lights.

THE CARRIER

CAPTAIN BIGGLESWORTH, of Squadron No. 266, R.F.C., sat shivering in the tiny cockpit of his Camel at rather less than 1,000 feet above the allied reserve trenches. It was a bitterly cold afternoon; the icy edge of the February wind whipped round his face and pierced the thick padding of his Sidcot suit as he tried to snuggle lower in his 'office'.

The little salient on his right was being slowly pinched out by a detachment of infantry; to Biggles it seemed immaterial whether the line was straightened out or not; a few hundred yards one way or the other was neither here nor there, he opined. He was to change his mind before the day was out. Looking down, he could see the infantry struggling through the mud from shell-hole to shell-hole, as inch by inch they drove the enemy back.

Squadron orders for the day had been to help them in every possible way by strafing back areas with machine-gun fire and 20-lb. Cooper bombs to prevent the enemy from bringing up reinforcements. He had been at it all morning, and as he climbed into his cockpit for the afternoon 'show', he anticipated another miserable two hours watching mud-coated men and lumbering tanks crossing no-man's-land, as he dodged to and fro through a venomous fire from small-arms, field-guns and archie batteries.

He was flying a zig-zag course behind the British lines, keeping a watchful eye open for the movements of enemy troops, although the smoke of the barrage, laid down to protect the advancing troops, made the ground difficult to see. It also served to some extent to conceal him from the enemy gunners. From time to time he darted across the line of smoke and raked the German front line with bullets from his twin Vickers guns. It was a highly dangerous, and, to Biggles, an unprofitable pursuit; he derived no sense of victory from the performance, and the increasing number of holes in his wings annoyed him intensely. 'I'll have one of those holes in *me* in a minute,' he grumbled.

Crash! Something had hit the machine and splashed against his face, smothering his goggles with a sticky substance.

'What's happened now?' he muttered, snatching off the goggles. His first thought was that an oil lead had been cut by a piece of shell, and he instinctively throttled back and headed the Camel nose down, farther behind his own lines.

He wiped his hand across his face and gave a cry of dismay as it came away covered in blood. 'My gosh! I'm hit,' he thought, and looked anxiously below for a suitable landing-ground. He had little time in which to choose, but fortunately there were many large fields handy, and a few seconds later the machine had run to a standstill in one of them. He stood erect in the cockpit and felt himself all over, looking for the source of the gore. His eye caught a sight of a cluster of feathers stuck on the centre section bracing wires, and he sank down limply, grinning sheepishly.

'Holy mackerel,' he muttered, 'a bird! So that was it!' Closer investigation revealed more feathers and finally he found a mangled mass of blood and feathers on the floor of the cockpit. 'The propeller must have caught it and chucked what was left of it back through the centre-section into my face,' he mused. 'Looks like a pigeon. Oh, well!'

He made to throw it overboard, when something

caught his eye. It was a tiny tube attached to the bird's leg.

'A carrier pigeon, eh?' He whistled. 'I wonder if it is one of ours or a Boche?'

He knew, of course, that carrier pigeons were used extensively by both sides, but particularly by the Allies for the purpose of conveying messages from spies within the occupied territory.

Sitting on the 'hump' of his Camel, he removed the capsule and extracted a small flimsy piece of paper. One glance at the jumbled lines of letters and numbers was sufficient to show him that the message was in code.

'I'd better get this to Intelligence right away,' he thought, and looked up to see an officer and several Tommies regarding him curiously from the hedge.

'Are you all right?' called the officer.

'Yes,' replied Biggles. 'Do you know if there is a field-telephone anywhere near?'

'There's one at Divisional Headquarters—the farm-house at the end of the road,' was the answer.

'Can I get through to 91st Wing from there?'

'I don't know.'

'All right; many thanks,' called Biggles. 'I'll go and find out. Will you keep an eye on my machine? Thanks.'

Five minutes later he was speaking to Colonel Raymond at Wing Headquarters, and after explaining what had happened, at the Colonel's invitation read out the message letter by letter. 'Shall I hold on?' asked Biggles at the end.

'No; ring off, but don't go away. I'll call you in a minute or two,' said the Colonel crisply.

Five minutes passed quickly as Biggles warmed himself by the office fire, and then the phone bell rang shrilly.

'For you, sir,' said the orderly, handing him the instrument.

'Is that you, Bigglesworth?' came the Colonel's voice.

'Yes, sir.'

'All right; we shan't want you again.'

'Hope I brought you good news,' said Biggles, preparing to ring off.

'No, you brought bad news. The message is from one of our fellows over the other side. The machine that went to fetch him last night force-landed and killed the pilot. That's all.'

'But what about the sp—man?' asked Biggles, aghast.

'I'm afraid he is in a bad case, poor devil. He says he is on the north side of Lagnicourt Wood. The Huns have got a cordon of troops all round him and are hunting him down with dogs. He's heard them.'

'How awful!'

'Well, we can't help him; he knows that. It will be dark in an hour and we daren't risk a night landing without looking over the ground. They'll have got him by tomorrow. Well, thanks for the prompt way you got the message to us. By the way, your M.C. is through; it will be in orders tonight. Goodbye.' There was a click as the Colonel rang off.

Biggles sat with the receiver in his hand. He was not thinking about the decoration the Colonel had just mentioned. He was visualizing a different scene from the one that would be enacted in mess that night when his name appeared in orders on the notice-board. In his mind's eye he saw a cold, bleak landscape of leafless trees through which crawled an unkempt, mud-stained, hunted figure, looking upwards to the sky for the help that would never come. He saw a posse of hard-faced, grey-coated Prussians holding the straining hounds on a leash, drawing ever nearer to the fugitive. He saw a grim, blank wall against which stood a blind-folded man—the man who had fought the war his own way, without hope of honour, and had lost.

Biggles, after two years of war, had little of the milk of human kindness left in his being, but the scene brought a lump into his throat. 'So they'd leave him there, eh?' he thought. 'That's Intelligence, is it?' He slammed the receiver down with a crash.

'What's that, sir?' asked the startled orderly.

'Go to blazes,' snapped Biggles. 'No, I didn't mean that. Sorry,' he added, and made for the door.

He was thinking swiftly as he hurried back to the Camel. 'North edge of Lagnicourt Wood, the Colonel said; it's nearly a mile long. I wonder if he'd spot me if I got down. He'd have to come back on the wing—it's the only way, but even that's a better chance than the firing party'll give him. We'll try it, anyway; it isn't more than seven or eight miles over the line.'

Within five minutes he was in the air heading for the wood, and ten minutes later, after being badly archied, he was circling over it at 5,000 feet.

'They haven't got him yet, anyway,' he muttered, for signs of the pursuit were at once apparent. Several groups of soldiers were beating the ditches at the west end of the wood and he saw hounds working along a hedge that ran diagonally into its western end. Sentries were standing at intervals on the northern and southern sides. 'Well, there's one thing I can do in case all else fails. I'll lay me eggs first,' he decided, thinking of the two Cooper bombs that still hung in their racks. He pushed the stick forward and went tearing down at the bushes where the hounds were working.

He did a vertical turn round the bushes at fifty feet, levelled out, and, as he saw the group just over the junction of his right-hand lower plane and the fuselage, he pulled the bomb-toggle, one—two. Zooming high, he half rolled, and then came down with both Vickers guns spitting viciously. A cloud of smoke prevented him from seeing how much damage had been done by the bombs. He saw a helmeted figure raise a rifle to shoot at him, fall, pick himself up, fall again, and crawl into the undergrowth. One of the hounds was dragging itself away. Biggles pulled the Camel up, turned, and came down again, his tracer making a straight line to the centre of the now clearing smoke. Out of the corner of his eye he saw other groups hurrying towards the scene, and made a mental note that he had at least drawn attention to himself, which might give the spy a chance to make a break.

He levelled out to get his bearings. Left rudder, stick over, and he was racing low over the wood towards the northern edge. At thirty feet from the ground he tore along the side of the wood, hopping the trees and hedges in his path. There was only one field large enough for him to land in; would the spy realise that, he wondered, as he swung round in a steep climbing turn and started to glide down, 'blipping' his engine as he came.

He knew that he was taking a desperate chance. A bad landing or a single well-aimed shot from a sentry when he was on the ground would settle the matter. His tail-skid dragged on the rough surface of the field; a dishevelled figure, crouching low, broke from the edge of the wood and ran for dear life towards him. Biggles kicked on rudder and taxied, tail up, to meet him, swinging round while still thirty yards away, ready for the take-off. A bullet smashed through the engine cowling; another struck the machine somewhere behind him.

'Come on!' he yelled frantically, although it was obvious that the man was doing his best. 'On the wing—not that—the left one—only chance,' he snapped.

The exhausted man made no answer, but flung himself at full length on the plane, close to the fuselage, and gripped the leading edge with his bare fingers.

'Catch!' cried Biggles, and flung his gauntlets on to the wing within reach of the fugitive.

Bullets were flicking up the earth about them, but they suddenly ceased, and Biggles looked up to ascertain the reason. A troop of Uhlans were coming down the field at full gallop, not a hundred yards away. Tight-lipped, Biggles thrust the throttle open and tore across the field towards them. His thumbs sought the Bowden lever of his Vickers guns and two white pencil lines of tracer connected the muzzles with the charging horsemen.

A bullet struck a strut near his face with a crash that he could hear above the noise of his engine, and he winced. Zooming high, he swung round towards the lines.

'I've got him—I've brought if off!' hammered exultantly through his brain. 'If the poor fellow doesn't freeze to death and fall off I'll have him home within ten minutes.' With his altimeter needle touching 4,000 feet, he pulled the throttle back and, leaning out of the cockpit, yelled at the top of his voice, 'Ten minutes!' A quick nod told him that the spy had understood.

Biggles pushed the stick forward and dived for the line. He could feel the effect of the 'drag'[1] of the man's body, but as it counterbalanced the torque[2] of his engine to some extent it did not seriously interfere with the performance of the machine.

He glanced behind. A group of small black dots stood out boldly against the setting sun. Fokkers!

'You can't catch me, I'm home,' jeered Biggles pushing the stick further forward.

[1] *'Drag': head resistance.*

[2] *Torque: the reaction of a propeller, which tends to turn an aeroplane in the opposite direction to which the propeller is turning.*

He was down to 2,000 feet now, his air-speed indicator showing 150 m.p.h.; only another two miles now, he thought with satisfaction.

Whoof! Whoof! Whoof! Three black clouds of smoke blossomed out in front of him, and he swerved. Whoof!—Spang! Something smashed against the engine with a force that made the Camel quiver. The engine raced, vibrating wildly, and then cut out dead. For a split second Biggles was stunned. Mechanically he pushed his stick forward and looked down. The German support trenches lay below.

'My gosh! What luck; I can't do it,' he grated bitterly. 'I'll be three hundred yards short.'

He began a slow glide towards the Allied front line, now in sight. At 500 feet, and fast losing height, the man on the wing twisted his head round, and the expression on his face haunted Biggles for many a day. A sudden thought struck him and an icy hand clutched at his heart.

'By heavens! I'm carrying a professed spy; they'll shoot us both!'

The ground was very close now and he could see that he would strike it just behind the Boche front line. 'I should think the crash will kill us both,' he muttered grimly, as he eyed the sea of shell-holes below. At five feet he flattened out for a pancake landing; the machine started to sink, slowly, and then with increasing speed. A tearing, ripping crash and the Camel closed up around him; something struck him on the head and everything went dark.

'Here, take a drink of this, young feller—it's rum,' said a voice that seemed far away.

Biggles opened his eyes and looked up into the anxious face of an officer in uniform and his late passenger.

'Who are you?' he asked in a dazed voice, struggling into a sitting position and taking the proffered drink.

'Major Mackay of the Royal Scots, the fust of foot, the right of the line and the pride of the British Army,' smiled his *vis-à-vis*.

'What are you doing here—where are the Huns?'

'We drove 'em out this afternoon,' said the Major, 'luckily for you.'

'Very luckily for me,' agreed Biggles emphatically.

SPADS AND SPANDAUS

BIGGLES looked up from his self-appointed task of filling a machine-gun belt as the distant hum of an aero engine reached his ears; an S.E.5, flying low, was making for the aerodrome. The Flight-Commander watched it fixedly, a frown deepening between his eyes. He sprang to his feet, the loose rounds of ammunition falling in all directions.

'Stand by for a crash!' he snapped at the duty ambulance driver. 'Grab a Pyrene, everybody,' he called; 'that fellow's hit; he's going to crash!'

He caught his breath as the S.E. made a sickening flat turn, but breathed a sigh of relief as it flattened out and landed clumsily. The visiting pilot taxied to the tarmac and pushed up his goggles to disclose the pale but smiling face of Wilkinson, of 287 Squadron.

'You hit, Wilks?' called Biggles anxiously.

'No.'

Biggles grinned his relief and cast a quick, critical glance at the machine. The fabric of the wings was ripped in a dozen places; an interplane strut was shattered, and the tail-unit was as full of holes as the rose of a watering-can.

'Have you got a plague of rats or something over at your place?' he inquired, pointing at the holes. 'You want to get some cats.'

'The rats that did that have red noses, and it'll take more than cats to catch 'em,' said Wilkinson meaningly, climbing stiffly out of the cockpit.

'Red noses, did you say?' said Biggles, the smile fading from his face. 'You mean—'

'The Richthofen crowd have moved down, that's what I mean,' replied Wilkinson soberly. 'I've lost Browne and Chadwicke, although I believe Browne managed to get down just over our side of the line. There must have been over twenty Huns in the bunch we ran into.'

'What were they flying?'

'Albatrosses. I counted sixteen crashes on the ground between Le Cateau and here, theirs and ours. There's an R.E.8 on its nose between the lines. There's a Camel and an Albatross piled up together in the Hun front-line trench. What are we going to do about it?'

'Pray for dud weather, and pray hard,' said Biggles grimly. 'See any Camels on your way?'

Wilkinson nodded. 'I saw three near Mossyface Wood.'

'That'd be Mac; he's got Batty and a new man with him.'

'Well, they'll have discovered there's a war on by now,' observed Wilkinson. 'Do you feel like making Fokker fodder of yourself, or what about running down to Clarmes for a drink and talk things over?'

'Suits me,' replied Biggles. 'I've done two patrols today and I'm tired. Come on; I'll ask the C.O. if we can have the tender.'

Half an hour later they pulled up in front of the Hôtel de Ville, in Clarmes. In the courtyard stood a magnificent touring car which an American staff officer had just vacated. Lost in admiration, Biggles took a step towards it.

'Thinking of buying it?' said a voice at his elbow.

Turning, Biggles beheld a captain of the American Flying Corps. 'Why, are you thinking of selling it?' he asked evenly.

As he turned and joined Wilkinson at a table, the American seated himself near them. 'You boys just going to the line?' he asked. 'Because if you are I'll give you a tip or two.'

Biggles eyed the speaker coldly. 'Are you just going up?' he inquired.

'Sure,' replied the American. 'I'm commanding the 299th Pursuit Squadron. We moved in today—we shall be going over tomorrow.'

'I see,' said Biggles slowly; 'then I'll give *you* a tip. Don't cross the line under fifteen thousand.'

The American flushed. 'I wasn't asking you for advice,' he snapped; 'we can take care of ourselves.'

Biggles finished his drink and left the room.

'That baby fancies himself a bit,' observed the American to Wilkinson. 'When he's heard a gun or two go off he won't be so anxious to hand out advice. Who is he?'

'His name's Bigglesworth,' said Wilkinson civilly. 'Officially, he's only shot down twelve Huns and five balloons, but to my certain knowledge he's got several more.'

'That kid? Say, don't try that on me, brother. You've got a dozen Huns, too, I expect,' jibed the American.

'Eighteen, to be precise,' said Wilkinson, casually tapping a cigarette.

The American paused with his drink halfway to his lips. He set the glass back on the table. 'Say, do you mean that?' he asked incredulously.

Wilkinson shrugged his shoulders, but did not reply.

'What did he mean when he said not to cross the line under fifteen thousand?' asked the American curiously.

'I think he was going to tell you that the Richthofen circus had just moved in opposite,' explained Wilkinson.

'I've heard of that lot,' admitted the American. 'Who are they?'

Wilkinson looked at him in surprise. 'They are a big bunch of star pilots each with a string of victories to his credit. They hunt together, and are led by Manfred Richthofen, whose score stands at about seventy. With him he's got his brother, Lothar—with about thirty victories. There's Gussmann and Wolff and Weiss, all old hands at the game. There's Karjust, who has only one arm, but shoots better than most men with two. Then there's Lowenhardt, Reinhard, Udet and—but what does it matter? A man who hasn't been over the line before meeting that bunch, has about as much chance as a rabbit in a wild-beast show,' he concluded.

'You trying to put the wind up me?'

'No. I'm just telling you why Biggles said don't cross under 15,000 feet. You may have a chance to dive home, if you meet 'em. That's all. Well, cheerio; see you later perhaps.'

'It's a thundering shame,' raved Biggles, as they drove back to the aerodrome. 'Some of these Americans are the best stuff in the world. One or two of 'em have been out here for months with our own squadrons and the French Lafayette and Cigognes Escadrilles. Now their brass-hats have pulled 'em out and rolled 'em into their own Pursuit Squadrons. Do they put them in charge because they know the game? Do they? No! They hand 'em over to some poor boob who has done ten hours' solo in Texas or somewhere, but has got a command because his sister's in the Follies; and they've got to follow where he leads 'em. Bah! It makes me sick. You heard that poor prune just now? He'll go beetling over at five thousand just to show he knows more about it than we do. Well, he'll be pushing up the Flanders poppies by this time tomorrow night unless a miracle happens. He'll take his boys with him, that's the curse of it. Not one of 'em'll ever get back—you watch it,' he concluded, bitterly.

'We can't let 'em do that,' protested Wilkinson.

'What can we do?'

'I was just thinking.'

'I've got it,' cried Biggles. 'Let them be the bait to bring the Huns down. With your S.E.s and our Camels together we'll knock the spots off that Hun circus. How many S.E.s can you raise?'

'Eight or nine.'

'Right. You ask your C.O. and let me know tonight. I'll ask Major Mullen for all the Camels we can get in the air. That should even things up a bit; we'll be strong enough to take on anything the Huns can send against us. I'll meet you over Mossyface at six. How's that?'

'Suits me. I hope it's a fine day,' yawned Wilkinson.

The show turned out to be a bigger one than Biggles anticipated. Major Mullen had decided to lead the entire Squadron himself, not so much on account of the possibility of the American Squadron being massacred, as because he realised the necessity of massing his machines to meet the new menace.

Thus it came about that the morning following his conversation with Wilkinson found Biggles leading his Flight behind the C.O. On his right was 'A' Flight, led by Mahoney, and on his left 'B' Flight, with MacLaren at their head. Each Flight comprised three machines, and these, with Major Mullen's red cowled Camel, made ten in all. Major Sharp, commanding the S.E.5. Squadron, had followed Major Mullen's example, and from time to time Biggles looked upwards and back- wards to where a formation of nine tiny dots, 6,000 feet above them, showed where the S.E.s were watching and waiting. A concerted plan of action had been decided upon, and Biggles impatiently awaited its consummation.

Where were the Americans? He asked himself the question for the tenth time; they were a long time showing up. Where was the Boche circus? Sooner or later there was bound to be a clash, and Biggles thrilled at the thought of the coming dog-fight.

It was a glorious day; not a cloud broke the serenity of the summer sky. Biggles kept his eyes downwards, knowing that the S.E.s would prevent molestation from above. Suddenly, a row of minute moving objects caught his eye, and he stared in amazement. Then he swore. A formation of nine Spads was crossing the line far below. 'The fools; the unutterable lunatics!' he growled. 'They can't be an inch higher than four thousand. They must think they own the sky, and they haven't even seen us yet. Oh, well, they'll wake up presently, or I'm no judge.'

The Spad Squadron was heading out straight into enemy sky, and Biggles watched them with amused curiosity, uncertain as to whether to admire their nerve or curse their stupidity. 'They must think it's easy,' he commented grimly, as his lynx-eyed leader altered his course slightly to follow the Americans.

Where were the Huns? He held his hand, at arm's length, over the sun, and extending his fingers squinted through the slits between them. He could see nothing, but the glare was terrific and might have concealed a hundred machines.

'They're there, I'll bet my boots,' muttered the Flight-Commander; 'they are just letting those poor boobs wade right into the custard. How they must be laughing!'

Suddenly he stiffened in his seat. The major was rocking his wings—pointing. Biggles followed the outstretched finger and caught his breath. Six brightly painted machines were going down in an almost vertical dive behind the Spads. Albatrosses! He lifted his hand high above his head, and then, in accordance with the plan, pushed the stick forward and, with Batson and Healy on either side, tore down diagonally to cut off the enemy planes. He knew that most of the Hun circus was still above, somewhere, waiting for the right moment to come down. How long would they wait before coming down, thus bringing the rest of the Camels and S.E.s down into the mix-up with them? Not long, he hoped, or he might find his hands full, for he could not count upon the inexperienced Spad pilots for help.

The Spad Squadron had not altered its course, and Biggles' lip curled as he realised that even now they had not seen the storm brewing above them. Ah, they knew now! The Albatrosses were shooting, and the Spads swerved violently, like a school of minnows at the sudden presence of a pike. In a moment formation was lost as they scattered in all directions. Biggles sucked in his breath quickly as a Spad burst into flames and dropped like a stone. He was among them now; a red-bellied machine appeared through his sights and he pressed his triggers viciously, cursing a Spad that nearly collided with him.

A green Albatross came at him head-on, and, as he charged it, another with a blue-and-white checked fuselage sent a stream of tracer through his top plane. The green machine swerved and he flung the Camel round behind it; but the checked machine had followed him and he had to pull up in a wild zoom to escape the hail of lead it spat at him.

'Strewth!' grunted Biggles, as his wind-screen flew to pieces. 'This is getting too hot. My gosh! what a mess!'

A Spad and an Albatross, locked together, careered earthwards in a flat spin. A camel, spinning viciously, whirled past him, and another Albatross, wrapped in a sheet of flame, flashed past his nose, the doomed pilot leaping into space even as it passed.

Biggles snatched a swift glance upwards. A swarm of Albatrosses were dropping like vultures out of the sky into the fight; he had a fleeting glimpse of other machines far above and then he turned again to the work on hand. Where were the Spads? Ah, there was one, on the tail of an Albatross. He tore after it, but the Spad pilot saw him and waved him away. Biggles grinned. 'Go to it, laddie,' he yelled exultantly, but a frown swept the grin from his face as a jazzed machine darted in behind the Spad and poured in a murderous stream of lead. Biggles shot down on the tail of the Hun. The Spad pilot saw his danger and twisted sideways to escape, but an invisible cord seemed to hold the Albatross to the tail of the American machine. Biggles took the jazzed machine in his sights and raked it from end to end in a long deadly burst. There was no question of missing at that range; the enemy pilot slumped forward in his seat and the machine went to pieces in the air.

The Spad suddenly stood up on its tail and sent two white pencils of tracer across Biggles' nose at something he could not see. A Hun, upside down, went past him so closely that he instinctively flinched.

'Holy smoke!' muttered Biggles. 'He saved *me* that time; that evens things up.'

His lips closed in a straight line; a bunch of six Albatrosses were coming at him together. Biggles fired one shot, and went as cold as ice as his gun jammed. Bullets were smashing through his machine when a cloud of S.E.s appeared between him and the Hun, and he breathed again.

'Lord, what a dog-fight,' he said again, as he looked around to see what was happening. Most of the enemy planes were in full retreat, pursued by the S.E.s. Two Camels and two Albatrosses were still circling some distance away and four more Camels were rallying above him. Biggles saw the lone Spad flying close to him. Seven or eight crashed machines were on the ground, two blazing furiously, but whether they were Spads or Camels he couldn't tell.

He pushed up his goggles and beckoned to the Spad pilot, whom he now recognised as his acquaintance of the previous day, to come closer.

The American waved gaily, and together they started after the Camels, led by Major Mullen's red cowling, now heading for the line.

Biggles landed with the Spad still beside him; he mopped the burnt castor-oil off his face and walked across to meet the pilot. The American held out his hand. 'I just dropped in to shake hands,' he said. 'Now I must be getting back to our field to see how many of the outfit got home. I'd like to know you better; maybe you'll give me a tip or two.'

'I can't tell you much after what you've seen today,' laughed Biggles, turning to wave to an S.E.5, which had swung low over them and then proceeded on its way.

'Who's that?' asked the American.

'That's Wilks, the big stiff you saw with me yester-day,' replied Biggles. 'He's a good scout. He'll be at the Hôtel de Ville tonight for certain; so shall I. Do you feel like coming along to tear a chop or two?'

'Sure,' agreed the Spad pilot enthusiastically.

THE ZONE CALL

Oh, my batman awoke me from my bed;
I'd had a thick night and I'd got a sore head;
   So I said to myself,
   To myself, I said,
Oh, I haven't got a hope in the mo-orning.

So I went to the sheds to examine my gun,
And then my engine I tried to run,
   But the revs she ga-ave.
   Were a thousand and one.
So I hadn't got a hope in the mo-orning.

THE words of the old R.F.C. song, roared by forty youthful voices to the tune of 'John Peel', drowned the accompaniment of the cracked mess piano in spite of the strenuous efforts of the pianist to make his notes audible.

Biggles pushed the hair off his forehead. 'Lord, it's hot in here; I'm going outside for a breath of air,' he said to Wilkinson of 287 Squadron, who had come over for the periodical party.

The two officers rose and strolled slowly towards the door. It was still daylight, but a thick layer of thunder-cloud hung low in the sky, making the atmosphere oppressive.

Oh, we were escorting 'twenty-two,'
Hadn't got a notion what to do,
   So we shot down a Spa-ad,
   And an S.E. too,
For we hadn't———

'Stop!' Biggles had bounded back into the centre of the room and held up his arms for silence. 'Hark!'

At the expression on his face a sudden hush fell upon the assembly, and the next instant forty officers had stiffened into attitudes of tense expectancy as a low vibrating hum filled the air. It was the unmistakable 'pour-vous' of a Mercédès aero-engine, low down, not far away.

'A Hun!' The silence was broken by a wild yell and the crash of fallen chairs as Biggles darted through the open door and streaked like a madman for the sheds, shouting orders as he went. The ack-emmas had needed no warning; a Camel was already on the tarmac; others were being wheeled out with feverish speed. Capless and goggleless, tunic thrown open at the throat, Biggles made a flying leap into the cockpit of the first Camel, and within a minute, in spite of Wilkinson's plaintive 'Wait for me', was tearing down-wind across the sun-baked aerodrome in a cloud of dust.

He was in the air, climbing back up over the sheds, before the second machine was ready to take off. The clouds were low, and at 1,000 feet the grey mist was swirling in his slipstream. He could no longer hear the enemy plane, for the roar of his Bentley Rotary drowned all other sound. He pushed his joystick forward for a moment to gather speed and then pulled it back in a swift zoom. Bursting out into the sunlight above he literally flung the machine round in a lightning righthand turn to avoid crashing into a Pfalz scout, painted vivid scarlet with white stripes behind the pilot's seat.

'My gosh!' muttered Biggles, startled. 'I nearly rammed him.'

He was round in a second, warming his guns as he came. The Pfalz had turned, too, and was now circling erratically in a desperate effort to avoid the glittering pencil lines of tracer that started at the muzzles of Biggles' guns and ended at the tail of the Boche machine. The German pilot made no attempt to retaliate, but concentrated on dodging the hail of lead, waving his left arm above his head. Biggles ceased firing and looked about him suspiciously, but not another enemy machine was in sight.

'Come on; let's get it over,' he muttered, as he thumbed his triggers again; but the Boche put his nose down and dived through the cloud, Biggles close behind him.

They emerged below the cloud bank in the same relative positions, and it at once became obvious that the German intended to land on the aerodrome, but a brisk burst of machine-gun fire from the Lewis guns in front of the mess caused him to change his mind; instead, he hopped over the hedge and made a clumsy landing in the next field. Biggles landed close behind him and ran towards the pilot, now struggling to get a box of matches from his inside pocket to fire the machine.

Biggles seized him by the collar and threw him clear.

'Speak English?' he snapped.

'Yes.'

'What's the matter with you? Haven't you got any guns?' sneered the British pilot, noting the German's pale face.

'Nein, no guns,' said the German quickly.

'What?'

The German shrugged his shoulders and pointed. A swift glance showed Biggles that such was indeed his case.

'Great Scott!' he cried, aghast. 'You people running short of weapons or something? We'd better lend you some.'

'I vas lost,' said the German pilot resignedly. 'I am to take a new Pfalz to Lille, but the clouds—I cannot see. The benzine is nearly finished. You come—I come down, so.'

'Tough luck,' admitted Biggles as a crowd of officers and ack-emmas arrived on the scene at the double. 'Well, come and have a drink—you've butted into a party.'

'Huh! No wonder your crowd scores if you go about shooting at delivery. pilots,' grinned Wilkinson, who had just landed.

'You go and stick your face in an oil sump, Wilks,' cried Biggles hotly. 'How did I know he hadn't any guns?'

Biggles sprang lightly from the squadron tender and looked at the deserted aerodrome in astonishment. It was the morning following his encounter with the un-armed Pfalz. For some days a tooth had been troubling him, and on the advice of the Medical Officer he had been to Clarmes to have the offending molar extracted. He had not hurried back, as the M.O. had forbidden him to fly that day, and now he had returned to find every machine except his own in the air.

'Where have they all gone, Flight?' he asked the Flight-Sergeant.

'Dunno, sir. The C.O. came out in a hurry about an hour ago and they all went off together,' replied the N.C.O.

'Just my luck,' grumbled Biggles. 'Trust something to happen when I'm away for a few hours! Oh, well!'

He made his way to the Squadron office, where he found Tyler, commonly known as 'Wat', the Recording Officer, busy with some papers.

'What's on, Wat?' asked Biggles.

'Escort.'

THE ZONE CALL 39

'Escorting what?'

'You remember that Hun you got yesterday?'

Biggles nodded.

'Well, apparently he was three sheets in the wind when Wing came and fetched him. He blabbed a whole lot of news to the Intelligence people. This is what he told 'em. He said that three new Staffels were being formed at Lagnicourt. A whole lot of new machines were being sent there; in fact, when he was there two days ago, over thirty machines were being assembled.'

'Funny, him letting a thing like that drop,' interrupted Biggles. 'He didn't strike me as being blotto, either. He drank practically nothing.'

'Well, Wing says he was as tight as a lord, and bragged that the three new circuses were going to wipe us off the map, so they decided to nip the plot in the bud. They've sent every machine they can get into the air with a full load of bombs to fan the whole caboodle sky-high—all the Fours, Nines, and Biffs[1] have gone, and even the R.E.8s they can spare from Art. Obs.[2] Two-eight-seven, two-nine-nine and our people are escorting 'em.'

'Well, they can have it,' said Biggles cheerfully. 'Escorting's a mouldy business, anyway. Thanks, Wat.'

He strolled out on to the aerodrome, gently rubbing his lacerated jaw, and catching sight of the German machine now standing on the tarmac made his way slowly towards it. He examined it with interest, for a complete ready-to-fly-away Boche machine was a *rara avis*. He slipped his hand into the map case, but the maps had been removed. His fingers felt and closed around a torn piece of paper at the bottom of the lining; it was creased as if it had been roughly torn off and used to mark a fold in a map. Biggles glanced at it disinterestedly, noting some typewritten matter on it, but as it

[1] *Bristol Fighters.* [2] *Artillery Observation.*

was in German and conveyed nothing to him he was about to throw it away when the Flight-Sergeant passed near him.

'Do you speak German, Flight?' called Biggles.

'No, sir, but Thompson does; he used to be in the Customs Office or something like that,' replied the N.C.O.

'Ask him to come here a minute, will you?' said Biggles.

'Can you tell me what that says?' he asked a moment later, as an ack-emma approached him and saluted.

The airman took the paper and looked at it for a minute without speaking. 'It's an extract from some orders, sir,' he said at length. 'The first part of it's gone, but this is what it says, roughly speaking: "With effect"—there's a bit gone there—"any flieger"—flyer, that is—"Falling into the hands of the enemy will therefore repeat that three Jagdstaffels are being assembled at Lagni———" Can't read the place, sir. "By doing so, he will be doing service by assisting"—can't read that, sir. It ends, "Expires on July 21st at twelve, midnight. This order must on no account be taken into the air." That's all, sir.'

'Read that again,' said Biggles slowly.

After the airman had obeyed, Biggles returned to the Squadron office deep in thought. He put a call through to Wing Headquarters and asked for Colonel Raymond.

'That you, sir? Bigglesworth here,' he said, as the Colonel's crisp voice answered him. 'About this big raid, sir. Do you mind if I ask whether you know for certain that these Boche machines are at Lagnicourt?'

'Yes; we made reconnaissance at dawn, and the observer reported several machines in various stages of erection on the tarmac. Why do you ask?'

'I've just found a bit of paper in the Pfalz that Boche

brought over. I can't read it because it's in German, but I've had it translated, and it looks as if that Hun had orders to tell you that tale. Will you send over for it?'

'I'll send a messenger for it right away, but I shouldn't worry about it; the Huns are there; we've seen them. Goodbye.'

Biggles hung the receiver up slowly and turned to Wat, who had listened to the conversation.

'You'll get shot one day ringing up the Wing like that!' he said reprovingly.

'It would be a deuce of a joke to send forty machines to drop twenty thousand quid's worth of bombs on a lot of obsolete spare parts,' mused Biggles. 'But there's more in it than that. The Boche want our machines out of the way. Why? That's what I want to know. Lagnicourt lies thirty miles north-west of here. I fancy it wouldn't be a bad idea if somebody went and had a dekko what the Huns were doing in the north-east. Even my gross intelligence tells me that when a Hun is told what he's got to say when he's shot down there's something fishy about it.'

'The M.O. says you're not to fly today,' protested the R.O.

'Rot! What the deuce does he think I fly with, my teeth?' asked Biggles sarcastically. 'See you later.'

Within ten minutes Biggles was in the air, heading into the blue roughly to the north-east of the aerodrome. An unusual amount of archie marked his progress and he noticed it with satisfaction, for it tended to confirm his suspicions.

'What ho!' he addressed the invisible gunner. 'So you don't want any Peeping Toms about today, eh? Want to discourage me.'

The archie became really hot, and twice he had to circle to spoil the gunner's aim. He kept a watchful eye on the ground below, but saw nothing unusual.

He passed over an R.E.8 spotting for the artillery, manfully plodding its monotonous figure-of-eight 3,000 feet below, and nodded sympathetically. Presently he altered his course a little westerly and the archie faded away. 'Don't mind me going that way, eh? Well, let's try the other way again,' he muttered. Instantly the air was thick with black, oily bursts of smoke, and Biggles nodded understandingly. 'So I'm getting warm, am I?' he mused. 'They might as well say so; what imaginations they've got.'

Straight ahead of him, lying like a great dark green stain across the landscape, lay the forest of Duvigny. Keeping a watchful eye above for enemy aircraft, he looked at it closely, but there was no sign of anything unusual about its appearance.

'I wonder if that's it?' he mused, deep in thought. 'I could soon find out; it's risky, but it's the only way.'

He knew what all old pilots knew, a trick the German pilots had learned early in the war, when vast numbers of Russian troops were concealed in the forests along the north-German frontier; and that was, that if an enemy plane flew low enough, the troops, no matter how well hidden, would reveal their presence by shooting at it. Not even strict orders could prevent troops from firing at an enemy aeroplane within range.

He pushed his stick forward and went roaring down at the forest. At 1,000 feet he started pulling out, but not before he had seen several hundred twinkling fireflies among the greenery. The fireflies were, of course, the flashes of rifles aimed at him. In one place a number of men had run out into a little clearing and started firing, but an officer had driven them back.

'So that's it, is it?' muttered Biggles, thrilling with excitement. 'I wonder how many of them there are.'

Time and time again he dived low over different parts of the forest and each time the twinkling flashes betrayed the hidden troops. His wings were holed in many places, but he heeded them not. It would take a lucky shot from a rifle to bring him down.

'My gosh!' he muttered, as he pulled up at the far end of the forest, after his tenth dive. 'The wood's full of 'em. There must be fifty thousand men lying in that timber, and it's close to the line. They're massing for a big attack. What did those orders say? July 21st? That's tomorrow. They'll attack this afternoon, or at latest tonight. I'd better be getting out of this. So that's why they didn't want any of our machines prowling about.'

He made for the line, toying with the fine adjustment to get the very last rev. out of his engine. He could see the R.E.8 still tapping out its 'G.G.' (fire) signal to the gunners and marking the position of the falling shells, and the sight of it gave him an idea. The R.E.8 was fitted with wireless; he was not. If only he could get the pilot to send out a zone call on that wood, his work was done.[1]

Biggles flew close to the R.E.8, signalling to attract attention. How could he tell them, that was the problem? He flew closer and gesticulated wildly, jabbing downwards towards the wood, and then tapping with his finger on an invisible key. The pilot and observer eyed him stupidly and Biggles shrugged his shoulders

[1] *A Zone Call was a special call from an aircraft to the artillery and was only used in very exceptional circumstances. When the zone call was tapped out by the wireless operator it was followed by the pin-point of the target. Military maps were divided into squares and smaller squares, each square numbered and lettered. By this means it was possible to name any spot on the map instantly. When a zone call was sent out, every weapon of every calibre within range, directed rapid fire on the spot, and this may have meant that hundreds of guns opened up at once on the same spot. The result can be better imagined than described. Obviously such treatment was terribly expensive, costing possibly £10,000 a minute while it lasted, and only exceptional circumstances, such as a long line of transport, or a large body of troops, warranted the call. There was a story in France of a new officer who, in desperation, sent out a zone call on a single archie battery that was worrying him. He was court-martialled and sent home.*

in despair. Then inspiration struck him. He knew the
morse code, of course, for every pilot had to pass a test in
it before going to France. He flew close beside the
R.E.8, raised his arm above his head and, with some
difficulty, sent a series of dots and dashes. He saw the
observer nod understandingly and grab a notebook to
take down the message. Biggles started his signal. Dash,
dash, dot, dot—Z, dash, dash, dash—O, dash, dot—N,
dot—E. He continued the performance until he had
sent the words, 'Zone Call, Wood,' and then stabbed
viciously at the wood with his forefinger. He saw the
observer lean forward and have a quick, difficult conversation with the pilot, who nodded. The observer
raised both thumbs in the air and bent over his buzzer.
Biggles turned away to watch the result.

Within a minute he saw the first shell explode in the
centre of the wood. Another followed it, then another
and another. In five minutes the place was an inferno of
fire, smoke, flying timber and hurtling steel, and thousands of figures, clad in the field-grey of the German
infantry, were swarming out into the open to escape the
pulverizing bombardment. He could see the officers
attempting to get the men into some sort of order, but
there was no stemming that wild panic. They poured
into the communication trenches, and others, unable to
find cover, were flinging away their equipment and
running for their lives.

'Holy mackerel, what a sight!' murmured Biggles.
'What a pity the Colonel isn't here to see it.'

A Bristol Fighter appeared in the sky above him,
heading for the scene of carnage. The observer was
leaning over the side and the pilot's arm was steadily
moving up and down as he exposed plate after plate in
his camera.

'He'll have to believe me when he sees those photographs, though,' thought Biggles. 'Well, I should think

I've saved our chaps in the line a lot of trouble,' he soliloquised, as he turned to congratulate the R.E.8 crew, but the machine was far away. Biggles' Camel suddenly rocked violently and he realised the reason for the R.E.8's swift departure. He was right in the line of fire of the artillery and the shells were passing near him. He put his nose down in a fright and sped towards home in the wake of the R.E.8.

He landed on the aerodrome to find the escorting Camels had returned, and the pilots greeted him noisily.

'Had a nice trip, chaps?' inquired Biggles.

'No,' growled Mahoney; 'didn't see a Hun the whole way out and home. These escorts bore me stiff. What have you been doing?'

'Oh, having a little fun and games on my own.'

'Who with?'

'With the German Army,' said Biggles lightly.

THE DECOY

BIGGLES landed and taxied quickly up to the sheds. 'Are Mr. Batson and Mr. Healy home yet?' he asked the Flight-Sergeant, as he climbed stiffly from the cockpit. 'We got split up among the clouds near Ariet after a dog-fight with a bunch of Albatri.'

'Mr. Healy came in about five minutes ago, sir; he's just gone along to the mess, but I haven't seen anything of Mr. Batson,' replied the N.C.O.

Biggles lit a cigarette and eyed the eastern sky anxiously. He was annoyed that his flight had been broken up, although after a dog-fight it was no uncommon occurrence for machines to come home independently. He breathed a sigh of relief as the musical hum of a Bentley Rotary reached his ears, and started to walk slowly towards the mess, glancing from time to time over his shoulder at the now rapidly approaching Camel. Suddenly he paused in his stride and looked at the wind-stocking.

'What's the young fool doing, trying to land cross-wind?' he growled, and turned round to watch the landing.

The Camel had flattened out rather too high for a good landing, and dropped quickly as it lost flying speed. The machine bumped—bumped again as the wheels bounced, and then swung round in a wide semi-circle as it ran to a standstill not fifty yards away.

Biggles opened his mouth to shout a caustic remark at the pilot, but his teeth suddenly closed with a snap, and the next instant he was running wildly towards the machine, followed by the Flight-Sergeant and several ack-emmas. He reached the Camel first, and, foot in the stirrup, swung himself up to the cockpit; one glance, and he was astride the fuselage and unbuckling the safety-belt around the limp figure in the pilot's seat.

'Gently, Flight-Sergeant, gently,' he said softly, as they lifted the stricken pilot from his seat and laid him carefully on the grass. Biggles caught his breath as he saw an ugly red stain on his hand that had supported the wounded pilot's back. 'How did they get you, kid?' he choked, dropping on to his knees and bending close over the ashen face.

'I — got — the — bus — home — Biggles,' whispered Batson eagerly.

'Sure you did,' nodded Biggles, forcing a smile. 'What was it, laddie—archie?'

The pilot looked at his Flight-Commander with wide-open eyes. 'My own fault,' he whispered faint-ly . . . 'I went down—after Rumpler—with green—tail. Thought I'd—be—clever.' He smiled wanly. 'Alba-trosses—waiting—upstairs. It was—trap. They got me —Biggles. I'm going—topsides.'

'Not you,' said Biggles firmly, waving away Batson's mechanic, who was muttering incoherently.

'It's getting dark early; where are you—Biggles——? I can't see you,' went on the wounded man, his hand groping blindly for the other pilot.

'I'm here, old boy. I'm with you; don't worry,' crooned Biggles, like a mother to an ailing child.

'Not worrying. Get that—Rumpler—for me—Biggles.'

'I'll get him, Batty; I'll get the swine, never fear,' replied Biggles, his lips trembling.

For a minute there was silence, broken only by the sound of a man sobbing in the distance. The wounded pilot opened his eyes, already glazed by the film of death.

'It's getting — devilish — dark — Biggles,' he whispered faintly, 'dev—lish—da—ark————'

The M.O. arrrived at the double and lifted Biggles slowly, but firmly, to his feet. 'Run along now, old man,' he said kindly, after a swift glance at the man on the ground. 'The boy's gone.'

For a moment longer Biggles stood looking down through a mist of tears at the face of the man who had been tied to him by such bonds of friendship as only war can tie.

'I'll get him for you, Batty,' he said through his teeth, and turning, walked slowly towards the sheds.

The Rumpler with the green tail was an old menace in the sky well known to Biggles. Of a slow, obsolescent type, it looked 'easy meat' to the beginner unaware of its sinister purpose, which was to act as a tempting bait to lure just such pilots beneath the waiting Spandau guns of the shark-like Albatrosses. Once, many months before, Biggles had nearly fallen into the trap. He was going down on to an old German two-seater when a premonition of danger made him glance back over his shoulder, and the sight that greeted his eyes sent him streaking for his own side of the line as if a host of devils were on his tail, as, indeed, they were.

Such death-traps were fairly common, but they no longer deceived him for an instant. 'Never go down after a Hun,' was the warning dinned into the ears of every new arrival in France by those who knew the pitfalls that awaited the unwary—alas, how often in vain.

So the old pilots, who had bought their experience, went on, and watched the younger ones come and go, unless, like Biggles, they were fortunate enough to escape, in which case the lesson was seldom forgotten.

. And now the green-tailed Rumpler had killed Batty, or had led him to his doom—at least, that was what it amounted to; so reasoned Biggles. That Batson had been deceived by the trap he did not for one moment believe. The lad—to use his own words—'tried to be clever', and in attempting to destroy the decoy had failed, where failure could have only tragic results; and this was the machine that Biggles had pledged himself to destroy.

He had no delusions as to the dangers of the task he had undertaken. Batson's disastrous effort was sufficient proof of that. First, he must find the decoy; that should not be difficult. Above it, biding their time, would be the school of Albatrosses, eyes glued downwards, waiting for the victim to walk into the trap.

Biggles sat alone in a corner of 'C' Flight hangar and wrestled with the problem, unconscious of the anxious glances and whispered consultations of his mechanics. The death of Batson had shaken him badly, and he was sick, sick of the war, sick of flying, sick of life itself. What did it matter, anyway, he mused. His turn would come, sooner or later, that was certain. He didn't attempt to deceive himself on that point. He made up his mind suddenly and called the Flight-Sergeant to him in tones that brooked no delay.

'Let's go and look at Mr. Batson's machine,' he said tersely.

'I have examined it, sir,' said the N.C.O. quickly. 'It's still O.K. Hardly touched; just one burst through the back of the fuselage, down through the pilot's seat and through the floor.'

'Good. I'll take it,' said Biggles coldly. 'Come and give me a swing.'

'But you're not going to—not going————?'

'Do what you're told,' snapped Biggles icily. 'I'm flying that machine from now on—until————' Biggles looked the flight-Sergeant in the eyes—'until—well, you know———' he concluded.

The N.C.O. nodded. 'Very good, sir,' he said briskly.

Five minutes later Biggles took off in the dead pilot's Camel; the Flight-Sergeant and a silent group of ack-emmas watched his departure. 'Mad as a 'atter. Gawd 'elp the 'Un as gets in 'is way today,' observed a tousle-headed Cockney fitter.

'Get back to your work,' roared the Flight-Sergeant. 'What are you all gaping at?'

Major Mullen hurried along the tarmac. 'Who's just taken off in that machine, Flight-Sergeant?' he asked curtly.

'Mr. Bigglesworth, sir.'

The C.O. gazed after the rapidly-disappearing Camel sadly. 'I see,' he said slowly, and then again, 'I see.'

The finding of the green-tailed Rumpler proved a longer job than Biggles anticipated. At the end of a week he was still searching, still flying Batson's mach-ine, and every pilot within fifty miles knew of his quest. Major Mullen had protested; in fact, he had done everything except definitely order Biggles out of the machine; but, being a wise man and observing the high pressure under which his pilot was living, he refrained from giving an order that he knew would be broken. So Biggles continued his search unhindered.

The Rumpler had become an obsession with him. For eight hours a day he hunted the sky between Lille and Cambrai for it, and at night, in his sleep, he shot it down in flames a hundred times. He had become mor-ose, and hardly even spoke to Mac or Mahoney, the other Flight Commanders, who watched him anxiously and secretly helped him in his search. He was due for leave, but refused to accept it. He fought many battles and, although he hardly bothered to confirm his victories, his score mounted rapidly. His combat reports were brief and contained nothing but the barest facts.

No man could stand such a pace for long. The M.O. knew it, but did nothing, although he hoped and prayed that the pilot might find his quarry before his nerves collapsed like a pack of cards.

One morning Biggles had just refuelled after a two-hour patrol, and was warming up his engine again, when a D.H.9 landed, and the observer hurried towards the sheds. Dispassionately, Biggles saw him speak to the Flight-Sergeant and the N.C.O. point in his direction. The observer turned and crossed quickly to the Camel.

'Are you Bigglesworth?' he shouted above the noise of the engine.

Biggles nodded.

'I hear you're looking for that green-tailed Rumpler?'

Biggles nodded again eagerly.

'I saw it ten minutes ago, near Talcourt-le-Chateau.'

'Thanks,' said Biggles briefly, and pushed the throttle open.

He saw the Rumpler before he reached the lines; at least, he saw the wide circles of white archie bursts that followed its wandering course. The British archie was white, and German archie black, so he knew that the plane was a German and from its locality suspected it to be the Rumpler. A closer inspection showed him that his supposition was correct. It was just over its own side of the lines, at about 8,000 feet, ostensibly engaged on artillery observation. Biggles edged away and studied the sky above it closely, but he could see nothing. He climbed steadily, keeping the Boche machine in sight, but making no attempt to approach it, and looked upwards again for the escorting Albatrosses which he knew were there; but he was still unable to discover them.

'If I didn't know for certain that they were there, I should say there wasn't a Hun in the sky,' he muttered, as he headed south-east, keeping parallel with the trenches. With his eye still on the Rumpler he could have named the very moment when the Boche observer spotted him, for the machine suddenly began to edge towards him as though unaware of his presence, and seemingly unconsciously making of itself an ideal subject for attack by a scout pilot.

To an old hand like Biggles the invitation was too obvious, and even without his knowledge of the trap the action would have made him suspiciously alert. Unless he was the world's worst observer, the man in the back seat of the black-crossed machine would not have failed to see him, in which case he should have lost no time in placing as great a distance as possible between himself and a dangerous adversary; for the first duty of a two-seater pilot was to do his job and get home, leaving the fighting to machines designed for the purpose. Yet there was an old and comparatively unmanoeuvrable machine deliberately asking for trouble.

'Bah!' sneered Biggles, peeved to think he had been taken for a fool. 'Will you step into my parlour?' said the spider to the fly. Yes, you hound, I will, but it won't be through the front door.'

He looked upwards above the Rumpler, but the sun was in his eyes, so he held on his way, still climbing, and had soon left the Boche machine far below and behind him.

At 15,000 feet Biggles started to head into enemy sky, placing himself between the sun and the Rumpler, now a speck in the far distance. His roving eyes suddenly focused on a spot high above the enemy plane.

'So there you are,' he muttered grimly. 'How many?

One—two—three'—he shifted his gaze still higher—
'four—five—six—seven. Seven, in two layers, eh?
Ought to be enough for a solitary Camel. Well, we'll
see.'

He estimated the lowest Albatrosses to be at about
his own height. The other four were a couple of thousand feet higher. With the disposition of the trap now
apparent he proceeded in accordance with the line of
action upon which he had decided. He had already
placed himself 'in the sun', and in that position it was
unlikely that he would be seen by any of the enemy
pilots. He continued to climb until he was above the
highest enemy formation, and then cautiously began to
edge towards them, turning when they turned and
keeping in a direct line with the sun.

He felt fairly certain that the crew of the Rumpler
would ignore the possibility of danger from above on
account of the escorting Albatrosses, and the pilots of
the enemy scouts would have their eyes on the machine
below. Upon these factors Biggles planned his attack. If
he was able to approach unseen he would be able to
make one lightning attack almost before the Huns were
aware of his presence. If he was seen, his superior
altitude should give him enough extra speed to reach
the lines before he was caught.

He knew he would only have time for one burst at the
Rumpler. If he missed there could be no question of
staying for a second attempt, for the Albatrosses would
be down on him like a pack of ravening wolves. The
Rumpler was now flying almost directly over no-man's-
land, and Biggles edged nearer, every nerve quivering
like the flying wires of his Camel.

The decoy, confident of its escort, was slowly turning
towards the British lines, and this was the moment for
which Biggles had been waiting, for the end of his dive
would see him over his own lines—either intact or as a

shattered wreck. His lips were set in a straight line under the terrific strain of the impending action as he swung inwards until the Albatrosses were immediately between him and the Rumpler, and then he pointed his nose downwards. 'Come on, Batty, let's go,' he muttered huskily, and thrust the stick forward with both hands.

The top layer of Albatrosses seemed to float up towards him. Five hundred feet, one hundred feet, and still they had not seen him; he could see every detail of the machines and even the faces of the pilots. He went through the middle of them like a streak of lightning—down—down—down—he knew they were hard on his heels now, but he did not look back. They would have to pull out as he went through the second layer—or risk collision.

'Come on, you swine,' he rasped through set teeth, and went through the lower Albatrosses like a thunderbolt.

The Rumpler lay clear below; he could see the observer idly leaning over the side of the fuselage watching the ground. He took the machine in his sights, but held his fire, for he was still too far off for effective shooting. Down—down—down—a noise like a thousand devils shrieking in his ears, his head jammed tight against the head-rest under the frightful pressure.

At 200 feet he pressed his triggers, and his lips parted in a mirthless smile as he saw the tracers making a straight line through the centre of the Boche machine. The observer leapt round and then sank slowly on to the floor of the cockpit. The nose of the Rumpler jerked upwards, an almost certain sign that the pilot had been hit.

Biggles held his fire until the last fraction of a second, and only when collision seemed inevitable did he pull the stick back. His under-carriage seemed to graze the

centre section of the Rumpler as he came out, and he bit
his lips until the blood came as he waited for the rending
crash that would tell him that his wings had folded up
under the pressure of that frightful zoom. Before he had
reached the top of it he had thrust the stick forward
again and was zig-zagging across his own lines.

For the first time since he had started that heart-
bursting dive he looked back. The Rumpler was
nowhere in sight, but an involuntary yell broke from his
lips as his eyes fell on two Albatrosses, one minus its
top-plane, spinning wildly downwards; whether as the
result of a collision or because they had cracked up in
the dive he neither knew nor cared. The five remaining
Albatrosses were already turning back towards their
own lines, followed by a furious bombardment of
archie.

Where was the Rumpler? He looked downwards. Ah!
He was just in time to see it crash behind the British
front-line trench. Tiny ant-like figures were already
crawling towards it, some looking upwards, waving to
him.

Biggles smiled. 'Given the boys a treat, anyway,' he
thought, as he pushed up his goggles and passed his
hand wearily over his face. A sound like a sob was
drowned in the drone of the engine. 'Well, that's that,'
he said to himself, and turned his nose for home.

The following morning, as the Sergeant-Major in
charge of the burying party at Lagnicourt Cemetery
entered the gate, his eye fell on a curious object that had
been firmly planted on a new mound of earth, at the
opposite end to the usual little white cross.

'What the devil's that thing, Corporal?' he said. 'It
wasn't there yesterday, I'll swear.'

The Corporal took a few steps nearer.

'That's where they planted that R.F.C. wallah last week, Sergeant-Major,' he replied. 'Looks to me like a smashed aeroplane propeller.'

'All right, let it alone. I expect some of his pals shoved it there. For-ward—ma—arch!'

THE BOOB

MAHONEY, on his way to the sheds to take his Flight off for an early Ordinary Patrol, paused in his stride as his eye fell on Biggles leaning in an attitude of utter boredom against the doorpost of the officers' mess.

'Why so pensive, young aviator?' he smiled. 'Has Mr. Cox grabbed your pay to square up the overdraft?' he added, as he caught sight of an open letter in the other's hand.

'Worse than that; much, much worse,' replied Biggles. 'Couldn't be worse, in fact. What do you think of this?' He held out the letter.

'I haven't the time to read it, laddie. What's the trouble?'

'Oh, it's from an elderly female relative of mine. She says her son—my cousin—is in the R.F.C. on his way to France. She's pulled the wires at the Air Board for the Pool to send him to 266, as she feels sure I can take care of him. She asks me to see that he changes his laundry regularly, doesn't drink, doesn't get mixed up with the French minxes, and a dozen other "doesn'ts." My gosh! it's a bit thick; what does she think this is—a prep. school?'

'What's he like?'

'I don't know, it's years since I saw him; and if he's anything like the little horror he was then heaven help us—and him. His Christian names are Algernon Montgomery, and that's just what he looked like—a slice of warmed-up death wrapped in velvet and ribbons.'

'Sounds pretty ghastly. When's he coming?'

'Today, apparently. His name's on the notice-board.

57

The old girl had the brass face to write to the C.O., and he's posted him to my Flight—in revenge, I expect.'

'Too bad,' replied Mahoney, sypmpathetically. 'Well, go and get the letter done, telling her how bravely he died, and forget about it. There comes the tender now—see you later.'

Biggles, left alone, watched the tender pull up and discharge two new pilots and their kit; he had no difficulty in recognizing his new charge, who approached eagerly.

'You're Biggles—aren't you? I know you from the photo at home.'

The matured edition of the youth was even more unprepossessing than Biggles expected. His uniform was dirty, his hair long, his face, which wore a permanent expression of amused surprise, was a mass of freckles.

'My name's Captain Bigglesworth,' said the Flight-Commander coldly. 'You are posted to my Flight. Get your kit into your room, report to the Squadron office, and then come back here; I want to have a word with you.'

'Sorry, sir,' said Algernon apologetically; 'of course, I forgot.'

A few minutes later he rejoined Biggles in the mess. 'What'll you have to drink?' invited Biggles.

'Have you any ginger ale?'

'I shouldn't think so,' replied Biggles. 'We don't get much demand for it. Have you any ginger ale, Adams?' he asked the mess waiter. 'I'll have the usual.'

'Yes, sir, I think I've got one somewhere, if I can find it,' replied the waiter, looking at the newcomer curiously.

'Sit down and let's talk,' said Biggles, when the drinks had been served. 'How much flying have you done?'

'Fourteen hours on Avros and ten on Camels.'

'Ten hours, eh?' mused Biggles. 'Ten hours. So they're sending 'em out here with ten hours now. My gosh! Now listen,' he went on; 'I want you to forget those ten hours. This is where you'll learn to *fly*—they can't teach you at home. If you live a week you'll begin to know something about it. I don't want to discourage you, but most people who come out here live on an average twenty-four hours. If you survive a week you're fairly safe. I can't teach you much; nobody can; you'll find things out for yourself. First of all, never cross the line alone under 10,000 feet—not yet, anyway. Never go more than a couple of miles over unless you are with a formation. Never go down after a Hun. If you see a Hun looking like easy meat, make for home, and if that Hun fires a Very light, kick out your foot and slam the stick over as if somebody was already shooting at you. Act first and think afterwards, otherwise you may not have time to act. Never leave your formation on any account—you'll never get back into it if you do, unless it's your lucky day; the sky is full of Huns waiting to pile up their scores and it's people like you that make it possible. Keep your eyes peeled and never stop looking for one instant. Watch the sun and never fly straight for more than two minutes at a time if you can't see what's up in the sun. Turn suddenly as if you've seen something—and you may see something. Never mind archie—it never hits anything. Watch out for balloon cables if you have to come home under 5,000. If a Hun gets on your tail, don't try to get away. Go for him. Try to bite him as if you were a mad dog; try to ram him—he'll get out of your way then. Never turn if you are meeting a Hun head-on; it isn't done. Don't shoot outside 200 feet—it's a waste of ammunition. Keep away from clouds, and, finally, keep away from balloons. It's suicide. If you want to commit suicide, do it here, because then someone else can have your bus. If you see anything you don't understand, let it alone; never let your curiosity get the better of you. If I wave my hand above my head—make for home. That means everybody for himself. That's all. Can you remember that?'

'I think so.'

'Right. Then let's go and have a look at the line and I'll show you the landmarks. If I shake my wings it means a Hun—I may go for it. If I do, you stay upstairs and watch me. If anything goes wrong—go straight home. When in doubt—go home, that's the motto. Got that?'

'Yes, sir.'

They took off together and circled over the aerodrome, climbing steadily for height; when his altimeter showed 6,000 feet Biggles headed for the line. It was not an ideal day for observation. Great masses of detached cumulus cloud were sailing majestically eastward and through these Biggles threaded his way, the other Camel in close attendance. Sometimes through the clouds they could see the ground, and from time to time Biggles pointed out salient landmarks—a chalk-pit—stream—or wood. Gradually the recognisable features became fewer until they were lost in a scene of appalling desolation, criss-crossed with a network of fine lines scarred by pools of stagnant water.

Biggles beckoned the other Camel nearer and jabbed downwards. Explanation was unnecessary. They were looking down at no-man's-land. Suddenly Biggles rocked his wings violently and pointed, and without further warning shot across the nose of the other Camel and dived steeply into a cloud. He pulled out underneath and looked around quickly, but of his companion

there was no sign. He circled the cloud, climbing swiftly, and looked anxiously to right and left, choked back
an expletive as his eye fell on what he sought. Far away,
almost out of sight in the enemy sky were five straight-
winged machines; hard on their heels was a lone machine with a straight top wing and lower wings set at a
dihedral angle—the Camel.

'The crazy fool!' ground out Biggles, as he set off in
pursuit; but even as he watched, the six machines disappeared into a cloud and were lost to view. 'I should
say that's the last anyone will see of Algernon Montgomery,' muttered Biggles philosophically, as he
climbed higher, scanning the sky in the direction taken
by the machines, but the clouds closed up and hid the
earth from view, leaving the lone Camel the sole
occupant of the sky. 'Well, I might as well go home and
write that letter to his mother, as Mahoney said,' mused
the pilot. 'Poor little devil! After all I told him, too.
Well————!' He turned south-west and headed for
home, flying by the unfailing instinct some pilots seem
to possess.

Major Mullen, MacLaren and Mahoney were standing on the tarmac when he landed. 'Where's the new
man, Biggles?' said Major Mullen quickly.

'He's gone,' said Biggles slowly as he took off his
helmet. 'I couldn't help it. I told the young fool to stick
to me like glue. We were just over the line when I
spotted the shadows of five Fokkers on the clouds; I
gave him the tip and went into the cloud, expecting him
to follow me. When I came out he wasn't there. I went
back and was just in time to see him disappearing into
Hunland on the tails of the five Fokkers. I spent some
time looking for him, but I couldn't find him. Could you
believe that a—bah!—it's no use talking about it. I'm
going for a dr——— Hark!' The hum of a rotary engine
rapidly approaching sent all eyes quickly upwards.

'Here he comes,' said Biggles frostily. 'Leave this to me, please, sir. I've something to say to him.'

The Camel landed and taxied in. The pilot jumped out and, with a cheerful wave of greeting, joined Biggles on the tarmac.

'I've———'

'Never mind that,' cut in Biggles curtly. 'Where do you think you've been?'

'I saw the Huns—I was aching to have a crack at them—so I went after them.'

'Didn't I tell you to stay with me?'

'Yes, but———'

'Never mind "but"; you do what you're told or I'll knock heck out of you. Who do you think you are—Billy Bishop or Micky Mannock, perhaps?' sneered Biggles.

'The Huns were bolting———'

'Bolting my foot; they hadn't even seen you. If they had you wouldn't be here now. Those green-and-white stripes belong to von Kirtner's circus. They're killers—every one of 'em. You poor boob.'

'I got one of them.'

'*You what?*'

'I shot one down. I don't think he even saw me, though. I got all tangled up in a cloud, and when I came out and looked up, his wheels were nearly on my head. I pulled my stick back and let drive right into the bottom of his cockpit. He went down. I saw the smoke against the clouds.'

Biggles subjected the speaker to a searching scrutiny. 'Where did you read that tale?' he asked slowly.

'I didn't read it, sir,' said the new pilot, flushing. 'It was near a big queer-shaped wood. I think I must have been frightfully lucky.'

'Lucky!' ejaculated Biggles sarcastically. 'Lucky! Ha, ha! Lucky! You don't know how lucky you are. Now listen. If ever you leave me again I'll put you under close arrest as soon as your feet are on the ground. Whatever happens, you stick to me. I've other things to do besides write letters of condolence to your mother. All right, wash out for today.'

Biggles sought Major Mullen and the other Flight-Commander in the Squadron office. 'That kid got a Hun or else he's the biggest liar on earth.'

'The liar sounds most likely to me,' observed MacLaren.

'Oh, I don't know; it has been done,' broke in Major Mullen; 'but it does seem a bit unlikely, I'll admit.'

The new pilot entered to make his report, and Biggles and MacLaren sauntered to the sheds. 'Wait a minute,' said Biggles suddenly. He swung himself into the cock-pit of the Camel which had been flown by the new pilot. 'Well, he's used his guns anyway,' he said slowly, as he climbed out again. 'I'll take him on the dawn patrol with Healy in the morning. He's not safe alone.'

Biggles, leading the other Camels, high in the early morning sky, pursed his lips into a soundless whistle as his eyes fell on a charred wreck at the corner of Mossy-face Wood.

'So he got him all right,' he muttered. 'The kid was right. Well, I'm dashed!'

A group of moving specks appeared in the distance. He watched them closely for a moment, then he rocked his wings and commenced a slow turn, pointing as he did so to the enemy machines which were coming rapid-ly towards them. He warmed his guns, stiffened a little in his seat, and glanced to left and right to make sure that the other two Camels were in place. He saw a flash of green-and-white on the sides of the enemy machines as they swung round for the attack, and he unconscious-ly half-glanced at the new pilot.

'You'll have the dog-fight you were aching for yesterday,' was his unspoken thought.

The Fokkers, six of them, were slightly above, coming straight on. Biggles lifted his nose slightly, took the leader in his sights, and waited. At 200 feet, still holding the Camel head-on to the other machines, he pressed his triggers. He saw the darting, jabbing flame of the other's guns, but did not swerve an inch. Metal spanged on metal near his face, the machine vibrated, and an unseen hand plucked at his sleeve. He clenched his teeth and held his fire. He had a swift impression of two wheels almost grazing his top plane as the first Fokker zoomed.

Out of the corner of his eye he saw Healy's tracer pouring into the Fokker at his right, and a trail of black smoke burst from the engine. Neither machine moved an inch. There was a crash which he could hear above the roar of his own engine as the Camel and the Fokker met head-on. A sheet of flame leapt upwards.

'Healy's gone—that's five to two now—not so good.'

He did a lightning right-hand turn. Where was Algernon? There he was, still in position at his wing-tip. The Huns had also turned and were coming back at them.

'Bad show for a kid,' thought Biggles, and on the spur of the moment waved his left hand above his head. The pilot of the other Camel was looking at him, but made no move.

'The fool, why doesn't he go home?' Biggles muttered, as he took the nearest Fokker in his sights again and opened fire. The Hun turned and he turned behind it, and the next second all seven machines were in a complete circle. Out of the corner of his eye Biggles saw the other Camel on the opposite side of the circle on the tail of a Hun.

'Why doesn't he shoot?' Biggles cursed blindly.

He pulled the stick back into his right side and shot into the circle, raking the Fokker that had opened fire on the other Camel. It zoomed suddenly, and as Biggles shot past the new pilot he waved his left arm.

He saw Algernon make a turn and dive for the line. A Fokker was on his tail instantly and Biggles raked it until it had to turn and face him. He half-rolled as a stream of lead zipped a strip of fabric from the centre section and went into a steep bank again to look at the situation.

He was alone, and there were still four Fokkers. For perhaps a minute each machine held its place in the circle, and then the Fokkers began to climb above him. Biggles knew that he was in an almost hopeless position, and he glanced around for a cloud to make a quick dash for cover, but from horizon to horizon the sky was an unbroken stretch of blue. The circle tightened as each machine strove to close it. The highest Fokker turned suddenly and dived on him, guns spitting two pencil lines of tracer. Biggles crouched a little lower in the cockpit. Two more of the Fokkers were turning on him now, and he knew that it was only a question of time before a bullet got him or his engine in a vital part.

Already the Camel was beginning to show signs of the conflict. 'Gosh! What's that?' Biggles almost stalled as another Camel shot into the circle. It did not turn as the others, but rushed across the diameter, straight at a Fokker which jerked up in a wild zoom to avoid collision. The Camel flashed round—not in the direction of the circle, but against it, and Biggles stared open-eyed with horror as the other Fokkers shot out at a tangent to avoid disaster.

'Great Scott! What's he doing?' he muttered as he flung his own machine on its side to pass the other Camel. He picked out a Fokker and blazed at it. Where were the others? They seemed to be scattered all over the sky. The other Camel was circling above him. 'We'll get out of this while the going's good,' he muttered grimly, and waved his hand to the other pilot. Together they turned and dived for the line.

Biggles landed first and leant against the side of his machine to await the new pilot. For a moment he looked at him without speaking.

'Listen, laddie,' he said, when the other had joined him. 'You mustn't do that sort of thing. You'll give me the willies. You acted like a madman.'

'Sorry, but you told me to go for 'em like a mad dog. I thought that's what I did.'

Biggles looked at the speaker earnestly. 'Yes,' he grinned: 'that's just what you did; but why didn't you do some shooting! I never saw your tracer once.'

'I couldn't.'

'Couldn't?'

'No—my gun jammed.'

'When?'

'It jammed badly with a bulged cartridge in that first go, and I couldn't clear it.'

Biggles raised his hand to his forehead. 'Do you mean to say you came back into that hell of a dog-fight with a jammed gun?' he said slowly.

'Yes. You said stick with you.'

Biggles held out his hand. 'You'll do, kid,' he said. 'And you can call me Biggles.'

THE BATTLE OF FLOWERS

THE summer sun was sinking in the western sky in a
blaze of crimson glory as Biggles, with his flying kit
thrown carelessly over his arm, walked slowly from the
sheds towards the officers' mess. At the porch he paused
in his stride to regard with wonderment the efforts of a
freckle-faced youth, who, regardless of the heat, was
feverishly digging up a small square patch of earth some
thirty feet in front of the mess door.

'What the deuce are you doing, Algy?' he called
cheerfully. 'Making a private dugout for yourself?'

'No,' replied Algernon Montgomery, straightening
his back with an obvious effort and wiping the per-
spiration off his brow with the back of his hand. 'I'm
making a garden. This dust-smitten hole wants
brightening up.'

'You're what?' cried Biggles incredulously.

'Making a garden, I said,' responded Algy shortly,
resuming his task.

'Good Lord! What are you going to sow, or whatever
you call it?'

'I've got some sunflowers,' replied Algy, nodding
towards a newspaper package from which some wilted,
sickly green ends protruded.

'Sunflowers, eh?' said Biggles, curiously, advancing
towards the scene of action. 'They ought to do well. But
why not plant some bananas or pineapples, or something we could eat?'

'It isn't hot enough for bananas,' said Algy, between
breaths. 'They were all I could get, anyway.'

'Not hot enough?' answered Biggles. 'Holy mackerel!

It feels hot enough to me to grow doughnuts.'

Algy dropped his spade and drew one of the seedlings gently from the package.

'Do you mean to tell me that you are going to stick that poor little thing in that pile of dust? I thought you said you were going to brighten things up,' said Biggles slowly.

'That'll be ten feet high presently,' said Algy confidently, scratching a hole in the earth and dropping the roots in.

'Ten feet! You mean to tell me that little squirt of a thing's got a ceiling of ten feet? Why, he's stalling already. Bah! You can't kid me. Straighten him up. You've got him a bit left wing low.'

'You push off, Biggles; I want to get these things in before dark,' cried Algy hotly. 'They've got to have some water yet.'

'They look to me as if a double brandy would do them more good,' retorted Biggles as he turned towards the mess. 'So long, kid—see you later. You can lie up in the morning. I'll take Cowley and Tommy on the early show.'

Three hours later Biggles pushed his chair back from the card-table in the anteroom. 'Well, I'm up five francs,' he announced, 'and now I'm going to roost. I'll———'

A voice from the doorway interrupted him. It was Algy.

'Here, chaps,' he called excitedly. 'Come and look at this—quick, before it goes.'

'He wants us to go and watch his posies sprouting in the moonlight, I expect,' grinned Biggles at Mahoney and MacLaren, who were leaning back in their chairs. He turned towards the door, but as his eye fell on a window which had been flung wide open to admit as much air as possible, he stopped abruptly. 'What the . . .?' he ejaculated, and sprang towards the door. The crash of falling chairs announced that the others were close behind him.

At the open doorway he stopped and looked up. A hundred feet above, a brilliant white light was sinking slowly earthwards, flooding the mess and the surrounding buildings with a dazzling radiance. A faint whistling sound, increasing in volume, became audible.

'Look out!' yelled Biggles and, covering twenty yards almost in a bound, dived headlong into a trench which surrounded a nearby Nissen hut. The whistle became a shrieking wail. 'Look where you're coming,' protested Biggles, as a dozen bodies thudded into the trench, one landing on the small of his back. 'Where's————?' His voice was lost in a deafening detonation; a blinding sheet of flame leapt upwards.

'If they've knocked my drink over————' snarled Mahoney, struggling to get out of the trench.

'Come back, you fool,' yelled Biggles, hanging on to his foot. 'Here comes another—get down.'

Bang! Another terrific explosion shook the earth, and falling debris rattled on the tin roof beside them. The roar of an aero-engine almost on their heads, but swiftly receding, split the air.

'All right, chaps, he's gone,' said Biggles, scrambling out of the trench. 'Don't step on my cigarette-case, anybody; I've dropped it somewhere. By thunder, he nearly caught us bending! To the deuce with these new parachute flares; they don't give you a chance.'

'I hope he hasn't knocked our wine store sideways, like somebody did to 55 the other day,' grumbled Mahoney. 'Hello! The searchlights have got him. Just look at that stinking archie; I wouldn't be in that kite for something.'

All eyes were turned upwards to where a black

crossed machine was twisting and turning in the beams
of three searchlights which had fastened upon it. The
air around was torn with darting, crimson jets of flame.

'He'll get away; they always do,' said MacLaren with
deep disgust, making his way towards the mess.

'Well, I hope he does; he deserves to. I'd hate his job,'
observed Biggles philosophically.

'Where's Algy?'

'I expect the kid's gone to see if his plantation's all
right,' replied Mahoney. 'Well, good night, chaps—
good night, Biggles.'

'Cheerio, laddie.'

Ten minutes later there was a knock on Biggles' door,
and in reply to his invitation a wild-eyed, freckle-faced
youth thrust his head inside. He seemed to be labouring
under some great emotion.

'What—what was that?' he gasped.

Biggles grinned. 'Hannoverana—didn't you see it in
the beam?' he replied. 'There's no harm done.'

'Where did that dirty dog come from, do you think?'
choked Algy.

'Aerodrome 29, I expect; they are the only Han-
novers near here. Must have crossed the line at twenty
thousand and glided down with his engine off,' replied
Biggles.

'Where's Aerodrome 29?'

'Oh, go to the map-room and find out; it's time you
knew. There are some photos there, too. Push off. I'm
tired and I'm on the early show.'

Algy stood for a moment breathing heavily, staring at
his flight-commander, and then abruptly slammed the
door.

Biggles scarcely seemed to have closed his eyes when
he was awakened by the ear-splitting roar of an engine.
It was still dark. He grabbed his luminous watch and

looked at the time—it was 3.30. 'What the dickens—?' he croaked, springing out of bed. He reached the window just as the dim silhouette of a Camel passed overhead. He flung on a dressing-gown and raced along the sun-baked path to the sheds. 'Who's that just gone off?' he called to a tousle-headed ack-emma who was still staring upwards with a vacant grin on his face.

'Alger—sorry, sir—Mr.———'

'Never mind,' snapped Biggles, overlooking the breach of respect. 'I know. Where's he gone—did he say?'

'No, sir, but I saw him marking up his map. He took eight Cooper bombs.'

'What did he mark on his map?' snapped Biggles.

'Aerodrome 29, sir.'

Biggles swung on his heel and tore back towards the huts. He shook and pummelled the life into Cowley and Thomas. 'Come on,' he said tersely; 'jump to it. Algy's gone off his rocker—he's shooting up 29 alone. Let's get away.'

Sidcots were hastily donned over pyjamas, and within five minutes three machines were in the air heading for the line. The sun was creeping up over the horizon when Biggles, at 5,000 feet, waved to the other two pilots and, leaning over the side of his cockpit, pointed downwards. Far below, a tiny moving speck was circling and banking over a line of hangars. A cloud of white smoke arose into the air. Tiny ant-like figures were running to and fro.

'The fool, the crazy lunatic!' gasped Biggles, as he pushed the stick forward and went roaring down with the others behind him.

At 500 feet a row of holes appeared like magic in his wing and he sideslipped violently. He levelled out and poured a stream of tracer at a group of figures clustered around a machine-gun. A green machine was taking off

cross-wind; he swung down behind it and raked it with
a stream of lead. The gunner in the rear seat dropped
limply and the machine crashed into the trees at the far
end of the aerodrome. The air was full of the rattle of
guns and an ominous *flack! flack! flack!* behind warned
him that it was time to be leaving.

He looked around for Algy, and, spotting him still
circling, zoomed across his nose, frantically waving his
arm above his head.

'If he doesn't come now he can stay and get what he
deserves,' muttered Biggles, as he shot over the edge of
the aerodrome.

He looked behind. To his relief three Camels were on
his tail, so, climbing swiftly for height, he headed back
towards the lines.

'I'll see him back home and then go straight on with
the morning show,' he mused a few minutes later as
they raced across the lines in a flurry of archie. He
landed and leaned against the side of the Camel while
he waited for the others to come in. Another Camel
touched its wheels gently on the aerodrome and finished its run not twenty yards away.

Algy sprang out of the cockpit and ran towards him.
'I got it—I got it!' he shouted exultantly as he ran.

'Who do you think you are?' snapped Biggles.
'Archimedes?'

'I got four hits out of eight,' cried Algy joyously.

'You got nothing—I had a good look. You didn't
touch a single hangar,' growled Biggles.

'Hangar—hangar—?' replied Algy stupidly. 'Who's
talking about hangars?'

'I am; what else do you suppose?'

'Hangars, be dashed!' cried Algy. 'I mean their
geraniums!'

'Germaniums—germaniums———? Am I going
crazy? What are you talking about—germaniums?'

'Raniums—raniums—N—N———! Good Lord, did you never hear of geraniums? They had a bed full of geraniums and calceolarias.'

'Calcium—calcium———' Biggles took a quick step backwards and whipped out his Very pistol. 'Here, stand back, you, or I'll shoot. You're daft.'

'Daft be dashed! I mean flowers—I've scattered their blinking geraniums all over the aerodrome.'

Biggles stared at him for a moment, his jaw sagging foolishly. 'Do you mean to tell me you've been to that hell-hole, and dragged me there, to bomb a perishing flower-bed?'

'Yes, and I've made a salad of their lettuce-patch,' added Algy triumphantly.

'But why? What have the lettuces done to you?'

'Done to me? Haven't you seen what that swine did to my sunflowers last night?'

Biggles swung round on his heel as enlightenment burst upon him. At the spot where Algy's flower-bed had been yawned a deep round hole.

THE THOUGHT-READER

THE summer sun blazed down in all its glory from a sky of cloudless blue. Biggles, his head resting on his hands, lay flat on his back in a patch of deep, sweet-scented grass in a quiet corner of the aerodrome, and stared lazily at a lark trilling gaily far above. The warmth, the drowsy hum of insects, and the smell of the clean earth were balm to his tired body. For since the disaster which had robbed his squadron of two thirds of its machines he had been doing three patrols a day. New Camels had now arrived, however, and at the commanding officer's suggestion he was taking things quietly for a few days.

The war seemed far away. Even the mutter of guns along the Line had died down to an occasional fitful salvo. France was not such a bad place, after all, he decided, as he glanced at his watch, and then settled himself again in the grass, his eyes on the deep-blue sky.

A little frown puckered his brow as he heard the soft swish of footsteps approaching through the grass, but he did not move. The footsteps stopped close behind him.

'You taking up star-gazing?' said a voice. It was Algy's.

'I should be if there were any to gaze at. You ought to know, at your age, that they only come out at night,' replied Biggles coldly.

'You'll be boss-eyed staring up that way,' warned Algy. 'Do you expect to see something, or are you just looking into the future?'

'That's it,' agreed Biggles.

'What's it?' asked Algy.

'I'm looking into the future. I can tell you just what you'll see up there in exactly three and a half minutes' time.'

'You're telling me!' sneered Algy. 'You mean a nice blue sky!'

'And something else,' replied Biggles seriously. 'I've been doing a bit of amateur astrology lately, and I'm getting pretty good at it. I can work things out by deduction. My middle name ought to have been Sherlock—Sherlock Holmes, you know, the famous detective!'

'Well, do your stuff,' invited Algy. 'What are you deducing now?'

Biggles yawned, and said: 'In one minute you'll see a Rumpler plane come beetling along from the south-east at about ten thousand feet. Our people will archie him, but they won't hit him. When he gets over that clump of poplars away to the right he'll make one complete turn, and then streak for home, nose down, on a different course from the one he came by.'

'This sun has given you softening of the brain,' declared Algy. 'What makes you think that, anyway?'

'I don't have to think—I know!' replied Biggles. 'I've got what is known as second sight. It's a gift that———'

'Come, come, Bigglesworth,' broke in another voice. 'You can't get away with that!'

Biggles raised himself on his elbow, and found himself looking into the smiling face of Colonel Raymond, of Wing Headquarters.

'Sorry, sir!' he gasped, struggling to get to his feet, 'I thought Algy was by himself.'

'All right—lie still, don't let me disturb you. I was just looking around—Hark!'

A faint drone became audible high overhead, and

three pairs of eyes turned upwards to a tiny black speck heading up from the south-east. Although small, it could be recognised as a German aeroplane, a Rumpler.

Whoof! Whoof! Whoof!

Three little fleecy white clouds blossomed out some distance behind it as the British anti-aircraft gunners took up the chase.

Biggles glanced at the others out of the corner of his eye, and their expressions brought a quick twitch of amusement to the corners of his lips. His smile broadened as the Rumpler held on its way until it was almost exactly above the group of poplars to which he had referred. Then, very deliberately, it made a complete circle and raced back, nose-down, towards the Lines on a different course.

'Not a bad forecast for an amateur!' observed Biggles calmly.

'Pretty good!' admitted Algy reluctantly. 'Maybe you know why he's flying in that direction now?'

'I do,' replied Biggles. 'It's a matter of simple deduction. He's going that way because if he followed his own course back he'd just about bump into Mahoney's flight coming in from patrol. He knows all about that, and as he doesn't fancy his chance with them he's steering wide of them.'

The enemy Rumpler was almost our of sight now, and the drone of its engine was gradually drowned by others rapidly approaching. Following the course by which the Rumpler pilot had crossed the Lines came three British Camels, straight towards the aerodrome.

'I told you my middle name ought to have been Sherlock!' grinned Biggles.

'Good show, Bigglesworth!' said the Colonel. 'I must say that was very neat. Tell us how you knew all this.'

'Oh, sir!' replied Biggles reprovingly. 'Fancy asking a

conjurer to show you how he does his tricks! It isn't done.'

'But I'm very interested,' protested the Colonel.

'So am I, to tell you the truth, sir!' Biggles replied. 'You know as much as I do now, but I figure it out this way. The average German hasn't very much imagination, and he works to a timetable, like a clock. I've been over here for the last two days at this time, and on both occasions that Rumpler has turned up and done exactly the same thing. Well, when I put my ear to the ground a little bird tells me that what a Hun does twice he'll do three times—and he'll keep on doing it until someone stops him. Maybe I shall have to stop him. If you ask me why he comes over here you've got me. I don't know. But I should say he comes over to look at something. He doesn't just come over on an ordinary reconnaissance. He's sent to look at something which he can see from that position where he turned over the poplars. Having seen it, he beetles off home. I may be wrong, but even my gross intelligence tells me he doesn't come over here just for fun. I must confess I'm getting a bit curious. What Huns can see I ought to be able to see.'

'That's what I was thinking,' agreed the Colonel. 'The Huns seem to be seeing quite a lot of this sector, too, of late. A week ago an artillery brigade took up a position in the sunken road at Earles. They were well camouflaged and could not have been seen from above, yet they were shelled out of existence the same night. That wasn't guesswork. We had to have some guns somewhere, so a couple of days ago we brought up a heavy naval gun, and sank it in a gun-pit behind that strip of wood on the Amiens road. It was perfectly concealed against aerial observation, yet by twelve noon the Boche artillery were raking that particular area and blew it to pieces. That wasn't guesswork,

either. Then some ammunition lorries parked behind
the walls of the ruined farm at Bertaple—the same
thing happened to them. Now you know what I mean
when I say that the Boche has been looking pretty
closely at this sector.'

'Someone's been busy, that's certain,' agreed Biggles.

'I wish you'd have a look round,' the Colonel went
on. 'I don't know what to tell you to look for—if I did,
there would be no need for you to go. You'll have to put
two and two together, and you're pretty good at that!'

'Don't make me blush in front of Algy, sir!' protested
Biggles, grinning. 'Right-ho; I'll beetle around right
away and see if I can see what the gentleman in the
Rumpler saw!'

Half an hour later, Biggles was in the air flying over
exactly the same course as that taken by the Boche
machine, and as he flew he subjected the ground below
to a searching scrutiny. Reaching the spot where the
Rumpler had turned, he redoubled his efforts, studying
the landscape road by road and field by field.

There was a singular lack of activity. Here and there
he saw small camps where British battalions from the
trenches were resting. He picked out a wrecked wind-
mill, minus its arms, an overturned lorry, and a
dispatch-rider tearing along a road in a cloud of dust.
One or two small shell-torn villages came within his
range of vision, and a farm-labourer harvesting his
corn, piling the sheaves into shocks, regardless of the
nearness of the firing-line. Shell-holes, both old and
new, could be seen dotted about the landscape, but he
could not see a single mark likely to be of interest to, or
which might be taken as a signal for, the enemy. He saw
the place, where the artillery brigade had been shelled,
and he turned away, feeling depressed.

For an hour or more he continued his quest, but
without noting anything of interest. And then, in not

too good a humour, he returned to the aerodrome.

Colonel Raymond was talking to Major Mullen when he landed.

'Well, Sherlock,' called the Colonel, 'what's the latest?'

'Nothing doing, sir,' replied Biggles shortly. 'But I haven't given up hope. I hope to pass the time of day with that Rumpler pilot tomorrow, anyway!'

The following morning he was in the air in ample time to intercept the Boche machine. In fact, he had deliberately allowed himself a wide margin of time in order to make a further survey of the ground which appeared to be the object of the enemy plane's daily visit, and towards which he now headed. Reaching it, he gave a grunt of annoyance as his probing eyes searched the earth below. Everything was just the same—the same lonely farm-labourer was still harvesting his corn.

Flying lower, he saw, farther on, a large body of British troops—a brigade, he judged it to be—lying fairly well concealed along the edge of a wood, no doubt awaiting their turn to move up to the trenches. He wondered vaguely whether the prying eyes in the Rumpler would see them, but he decided not, both from the fact that the machine would be too high up and would hardly be likely to venture so far over the British Line.

He glanced at the watch on his instrument-board and saw that he still had a quarter of an hour to wait for the Rumpler, assuming it came at the same time as before.

'Well, I might as well be getting plenty of height,' he mused, as he tilted the nose of the Camel upwards, glancing down for a final survey of the ground as he did so.

His eye fell on the labourer, still working at his harvest. It seemed to Biggles that he was working unnecessarily fast, and a frown lined his brow as he looked around the sky to see if there were any signs of an impending storm to account for the man's haste. But the sky was an unbroken blue canopy from horizon to horizon. He looked back at the man on the ground, and, leaning over the side of the cockpit to see better, he stared at the field and the position of the shocks of corn with a puzzled expression on his face. It struck him that, in spite of the man's haste in moving the corn, the shocks were as numerous as they had been the previous day. They only seemed to have moved their positions, and they now formed a curious pattern, quite different from the usual orderly rows.

'So that's your game, is it?' Biggles muttered, after a quick intake of breath, as he realised the significance of what he saw.

His eyes followed a long line of sheaves pointing in the direction of the concealed infantry, and a number of isolated shocks which probably indicated the distance they were away, and so disclosed their position to the German aerial observer!

Biggles' brain raced swiftly. What should he do? There were several courses open to him. He might proceed with his original plan and shoot down the Rumpler. That would at least prevent the information from reaching the German gunners.

But suppose he failed? Suppose the Boche shot him down? He did not anticipate such a catastrophe, nor did he think it likely, but it was a possibility. His engine might be damaged, when he would be forced to land, in which case there was nothing to prevent the Rumpler from reaching home. He might have engine trouble and have to force-land, anyway, and he shuddered to think of the consequences, for he had not the slightest doubt but that the British infantry would be annihilated by the guns of the German artillery.

Another plan would be to return to the aerodrome, ring up Colonel Raymond, at Wing Headquarters, and tell him what he had discovered. The Colonel could then send a message to the brigade warning them to shift their position before the bombardment started.

'No,' he decided: 'that won't do.' It would take too long. It would allow the Boche plane ample time to return home and start the enemy gunners on their deadly work before the message could reach the brigade.

The only really sure plan seemed to be to land and destroy the tell-tale signal before the Boche plane came over. If he could do that quickly he might still have time to get off again and get the Rumpler when it arrived.

'Yes,' he thought; 'that's the safest way!' There was still ten minutes to go before the Rumpler was due to appear on the scene.

Having made up his mind, he sideslipped steeply towards the ground near to where the supposed peasant was at work. The fact that he was unarmed did not worry him. After all, there was no reason to suppose that the spy would suspect he had been discovered—his method of conveying information to the enemy was so simple and so natural that nothing but a fluke or un-canny perception could detect it.

It was improbable that a roving scout pilot would even pass over the field so far behind the Lines, much less suspect the sinister scheme. But the improbable had happened, and Biggles, as he swooped earthwards, could not help admiring the ingenuity of the plan.

He did not risk a landing on the stubble of the cornfield, but dropped lightly to earth on a pasture a short distance away. Climbing from the cockpit, he threw his heavy flying-coat across the lower wing and started off at a steady trot towards the cornfield. As he neared it he slowed down to a walk in order not to alarm the spy, and made for a gate leading into the field. He saw the supposed labourer, dressed in the typical blue garb of a French peasant, still carrying the sheaves of corn, and he smiled grimly at his thoroughness. For the labourer did not so much as glance up when a distant deep-toned hum announced the approach of his confederate, the Rumpler.

He saw Biggles coming towards him and waved gaily.

'*Bonjour, m'sieur le capitan!*'he cried, smiling, and the pilot was too far away to see the curious gleam in his eyes.

'*Bonjour, m'sieur!*'echoed Biggles, still advancing.

He was still about twenty yards away when he saw the peasant's hand move quickly to his pocket, and then up. Before he even suspected the other's purpose, a deafening roar filled Biggles' ears, and the world seemed to blow up in a sheet of crimson and orange flame that slowly turned to purple and then to black.

As he pitched forward limply on his face, Biggles knew that the spy had shot him!

Biggles' first conscious realisation as he opened his eyes was a shocking headache. He tried to raise his arm to his head to feel the extent of the damage done by the spy's bullet, but his arm seemed to be pinned to his side. It was dark, too, and an overwhelming smell of fresh straw filled his nostrils, seeming to suffocate him. He saw some narrow strips of daylight in the darkness, and it took him several minutes of concentrated thought to realise that he was buried under a pile of corn-sheaves.

With a mighty effort that seemed to burst his aching head, he flung the sheaves aside and rolled out into the open, blinking like an owl in the dazzling sunlight. He struggled to his feet, and, swaying dizzily, looked about him. Apparently he was at the very spot where he had fallen; everything was precisely the same except that the spy had just flung the sheaves of corn over the pilot's unconscious body to conceal it from any casual passers-by, and then had made his escape.

Biggles wondered how long he had been unconscious, for he had no means of knowing; his watch was on the instrument-board of the Camel. From the position of the sun, however, he decided that it could not have been very long, but ample for the Rumpler pilot to read the message and return. At least, the machine was nowhere in sight, and he could not hear the sound of its engine. He tried to think, raising his hand to his aching head and looking aghast at his red-stained fingers when he took it away.

Suddenly he remembered the infantry, and with a shock he recalled the perilous position in which they must now be placed. He must get in touch with the brigade, was the thought that hammered through his brain. The inevitable artillery bombardment had not yet started, and he might still be in time to save them!

The sudden splutter of a motor-car engine made him swing round, and he was just in time to see a rather dilapidated old Renault car, with the spy at the wheel, disappearing out of the yard of the small farmhouse a short distance away, to which the cornfield evidently belonged. At the same time a thick column of smoke began to rise from the farm itself, and he guessed that they spy had set fire to the place to destroy any incriminating documents or clues he might have left behind in his hurried departure.

Biggles' lips set in a straight line, and his eyes narrowed.

'You aren't getting away with that!' he snarled, and started off at a swaying run towards the place where he had left his Camel, breathing a sigh of relief when he saw it was still there.

He paused for an instant at a ditch to soak his handkerchief and bind it round the place on the side of his head where the spy's bullet had grazed it.

'If I ever get a closer one than that it will be the last!' he muttered grimly, as he realized what a close shave he had had. Indeed, the spy must have thought he had killed him, he reflected, or he would not have left him to tell the tale.

He climbed into the cockpit, and, after a swerving run, somehow managed to get the machine off the ground and headed towards the road down which the spy had disappeared. He saw the car presently, and the long cloud of dust hanging in the air behind it, and he flung the Camel at it viciously, knowing that he had no time to lose. He knew he ought to go straight to the infantry brigade and sound the warning, but his blood was up and he could not bear to think the spy might escape to continue his dangerous work elsewhere. In any case, he thought, as he tore down the road just above the column of dust, the Rumpler pilot could scarcely have reached home yet, for the fact that he—Biggles—had caught the spy in the act of escaping indicated that he had not been unconscious for more than a few minutes. His lips parted in a mirthless smile as he saw the fugitive look back over his shoulder at the pursuing demon on his trail, and the car leaped forward as the spy strove to escape by increasing his speed.

Biggles laughed. The idea of any vehicle on the ground leaving his Camel, which was doing 140 miles an hour, struck him as funny. But the smile gave way to the cold calculating stare of the fighting airman as the Camel drew swiftly into range, and Biggles' eyes sought his sights.

Rat-tat-tat-tat-tat-tat! The twin Vickers guns began their song. The end came suddenly. Whether he hit the driver, or burst a tyre, or whether it was simply the result of the driver trying to take a bend at excessive speed, Biggles did not know, nor did he stop to ascertain. The car seemed suddenly to plough into the road, and a great cloud of dust arose above it. The bodywork, with a deliberation that was appalling to watch, seemed slowly to spread itself over the landscape. A solitary wheel went bounding along the road. A tongue of flame licked out of the engine, and in a moment all that was left of the wreck was concealed under a cloud of smoke.

Biggles grimaced at the unpleasant sight, and circled twice to see if by some miracle the driver was still alive. But there was a significant lack of movement near the car, and he shot off at a tangent in the direction of the infantry encampment.

He had made a bad landing, excusable in the circumstances, in an adjacent field, and ran quickly towards a group of officers whom he saw watching him.

'I must speak to the Brigadier at once!' he cried, as he reached them.

'Did no one teach you how to salute?' thundered an officer who wore a major's crown on his sleeve.

Biggles flushed, and raised his hand smartly to the salute, inwardly fuming at the delay.

'I must speak to the Brigadier or the Brigade-major at once!' he repeated impatiently.

A major, wearing on his collar the red tabs of a staff-officer, hurried up and asked: 'Are you the officer who just flew low over——'

'Do you mind leaving that until later, sir?' ground out Biggles. 'I've come to tell you to move your men at once. I——'

'Silence! Are you giving *me* orders?' cried the Brigade-major incredulously. 'I'll report you for impertinence!'

Biggles groaned, then had an inspiration.

'May I use your telephone, sir? It's very urgent!' he asked humbly.

'You'll find one at Headquarters—this way!'

In the Brigade Headquarters, Biggles grabbed the telephone feverishly. The Brigade-major and an orderly-officer watched him curiously. In a few moments he was speaking to Colonel Raymond at Wing Headquarters.

'Bigglesworth here, sir!' he said tersely. 'I've found what you were looking for. That Boche came over to pick up a message from a spy who has signalled to the German gunners the position of the brigade from whose headquarters I am now speaking—yes, sir— that's right—by the side of the wood about two miles east of Buell. Yes, I've tried to tell the people here, but they won't listen. I killed the spy—he's lying under the wreckage of his own car on the Amiens road. Yes, sir—I should say the bombardment is due to start any minute.'

'What's that—what's that?' cried a voice behind him.

Biggles glanced over his shoulder and saw the Brigadier watching him closely.

'Just a moment, sir,' he called into the telephone, and then, to the Brigadier: 'Will you speak to Colonel Raymond, of 51st Wing Headquarters, sir?'

The Brigadier took the instrument and placed the receiver to his ear. Biggles saw his face turn pale. An instant later he had slammed down the receiver and ripped out a string of orders. Orderlies dashed off in all directions, bugles sounded, and sergeant-majors shouted.

Ten minutes later, as the tail of the column disappeared behind a fold in the ground to the rear, the first shell arrived. A salvo followed. Presently the earth where the British camp had been was being torn and ploughed by flame and hurtling metal.

Biggles ran through the inferno of flying earth and

shrapnel to where he had left the Camel. The pain in his head, forgotten in the excitement, had now returned with greater intensity, and as he ran he shut his eyes tightly, fighting back the wave of dizziness which threatened him.

'I must have been barmy to leave the bus as close as this,' he thought. 'She's probably been blown sky-high by this time.'

There was reason for his concern, for the enemy shells were falling uncomfortably near the field where he had left the machine. But the Camel was intact when he reached it, although the ploughed-up ground which he had looked upon as a possible take-off showed how narrowly some of the shells had missed it.

Biggles scrambled into the cockpit and revved up the engine, then kicked hard at the rudder-bar to avoid the edge of a shell-hole as the machine lurched forward. Bumping and swaying on the torn ground, the Camel gathered speed.

'I'll have the undercarriage collapsing if I can't get off soon,' Biggles muttered, and eased back the joystick.

For a few moments the wheels jolted on the rough earth, then a bump bigger than usual threw them into the air.

As he landed at Maranique, Wat Tyler, the Recording Officer, handed him a signal.

'From Wing,' he said. 'What have you been up to now?'

Biggles tore the envelope open and smiled as he read: 'Good work, Sherlock!' The initials below were Colonel Raymond's.

BIGGLES FINDS HIS FEET

CRUISING over the Somme, France, at fifteen thousand feet, Biggles paused for a moment in his unceasing scrutiny of the sky to glance downwards. The smoke from a burning farmhouse caught his eye, and a little frown of anxiety lined his forehead as he noticed that the smoke was rolling along the ground towards Germany at an angle which could only mean that a very high wind was blowing.

He swung his Camel round in its own length, the frown deepening with anxiety as he realised for the first time that he was a good deal farther over the Lines than he imagined.

'It'll take me half an hour to get back against this wind. I must have been crazy to come so far over,' he thought, as he pushed his joystick forward for more speed.

The archie bursts that had followed him on his outward passage with indifferent results now began to creep closer as the Camel offered a less fleeting target. The pilot was forced to change direction in order to avoid their unwelcome attentions.

'I must have been crazy,' he told himself again angrily, as he swerved to avoid a cluster of ominous black bubbles that had appeared like magic in front of him. 'I ought to have spotted that the wind had got up. But how was I to know it was going to blow a gale?'

Under the forward pressure on the joystick, his height had dropped to ten thousand feet by the time the white scars of the shell-torn trenches came into view. Suddenly he stiffened in his seat as a faint but unusual noise reached his ears. Underlying the rhythmic hum of his Bentley engine was a persistent *tick-a-tack—tick-a-tack*.

With a grim suspicion forming in his mind, he glanced back over his shoulder. Along his line of flight, stretching away behind him like the wake of a ship, was a cloud of pale-blue smoke, and he knew beyond doubt that his engine was giving trouble.

He turned quickly to his instrument-board and confirmed it. The engine revolution counter had fallen to nearly half its normal revs. He looked over the side, now thoroughly alarmed, to judge his distance from the Lines. He decided, with a sigh of relief, that he might just reach them provided the trouble did not become worse. But in this he was doomed to disappointment, for hardly had the thought crossed his mind than there was a loud explosion, a streamer of flame leapt backwards from the whirling rotary engine, and a smell of burning oil filled his nostrils. Instantly he throttled back, preferring to land behind the German Lines rather than be burnt to a cinder in the air.

He lost height rapidly, and fixed his eyes on the Lines in an agony of suspense. Fortunately, the sky was clear of enemy machines, a fact which afforded him some consolation, for he would have been in a hopeless position had he been attacked.

Still gliding, he moistened his lips, and tried opening the throttle a trifle. But the flames reappeared at once, and he had no alternative but to resume his former gliding angle.

The Lines were not much more than a mile away now, but his height was less than a thousand feet, a fact that was unpleasantly impressed upon him by the closeness of the anti-aircraft gun-fire. An ominous crackling, too, warned him that the enemy machine-gunners on the ground were also making good shooting at the struggling machine. To make matters worse, there seemed to be a battle raging below. Clouds of smoke, stabbing spurts of flame, and leaping geysers of mud told a story of concentrated bombardment on both sides of the Lines. More than once the Camel rocked violently as a big projectile from the thundering howitzers hurtled by.

Biggles crouched a little lower in the cockpit, looking swiftly left and right, hoping to ascertain his position. But he was now too low to distinguish anything except the churning inferno of smoke and mud. A battered tank, its nose pointing upwards like that of a sleeping lizard, loomed up before him and he kicked the rudder desperately to avoid it. Barbed wire, tangled and twisted, was everywhere. Mud, water, and bodies in khaki and field-grey were the only other things he could see.

There was no question of choosing a place to land—everywhere was the same, so there was no choice. There came a deafening explosion, the Camel twisted into a sickening side-slip, and, with a crash of rending timbers, struck the upright post of some wire entanglements.

Biggles' next conscious recollection was of digging feverishly in the mud under the side of his now upside-down machine in order to get clear, and then staring stupidly at the inferno raging about him. In which direction lay the British Lines? He had no idea, but the vicious rattle of a machine-gun from somewhere near at hand, and the shrill whang of bullets striking his machine, brought him back from his semi-stunned condition with a rush, and suggested the immediate need for cover.

About twenty yards away a huge shell-crater yawned invitingly, and he leapt towards it like a tiger. A bullet clutched at the sleeve of his coat as he plunged through the mud, and he took the last two yards in a wild leap.

His foot caught on the serrated rim of the crater and he dived headlong into the stagnant pool of slime at the bottom. Scrambling out blindly, he slipped and fell heavily on something soft.

'Now, then, look where you're comin' to, can't you! What's the 'urry?' snarled a Cockney voice.

Biggles blinked and wilted into a sitting position in the soft mud on the side of the hole. On the opposite side sat a Tommy, caked with mud from head to foot, a drab and sorry spectacle; upon his knee, from which he had cut away a portion of his trousers, was a red-stained bandage which he had evidently just finished tying.

'Was I in a hurry?' inquired Biggles blandly, regarding the apparition curiously. 'Well, I may have been,' he confessed. 'This isn't the sort of place to dawdle on an afternoon's stroll—at least, it didn't strike me like that. Where are we, and what's going on?' he asked, ducking instinctively as a shell landed just outside the crater with a dull *whoosh*.

'What did you want to land 'ere for? Ain't it bad enough upstairs?' snorted the Tommy. 'Life won't be worth livin' 'ere in 'arf a minute, when they start puttin' the kybosh on your aeroplane.'

'I didn't land here because I was pining to see you, so don't get that idea,' grinned Biggles. 'Where are we— that's what I want to know.'

'About in the middle, I should think,' growled the Tommy.

'Middle of what?' asked Biggles.

'The war, of course!' was the reply.

'Yes, I can see that,' admitted Biggles. 'But whereabouts are our troops, and where's the enemy?'

The soldier jerked his thumb over his shoulder and then jabbed it in the opposite direction.

'There and there, or they was last time I saw 'em, but they might be anywhere by now. You know, mate, my missus, she says to me, "Bert," she says———'

'Is your name Bert?' asked Biggles, to stop the long oration he could see was coming.

'Yes. Bert Smart, 'A' Company, Twenty-third London,' replied the soldier.

'Nice name!' said Biggles.

'What's the matter with it?' growled the Tommy.

'Nothing! I said it was a nice name—nice and easy to remember!' protested Biggles.

'I thought you was pulling my leg!' growled Bert suspiciously.

'Oh, no, I wouldn't do that!' exclaimed Biggles, repressing a smile with difficulty. 'But what about getting out of here?'

'Well, I ain't stoppin' you, am I?' said Bert. 'If you don't like my blinkin' society———'

'It isn't that!' broke in Biggles quickly, a broad grin on his face. 'I'd like to sit and chat to you all day—but not here!'

'Well, it's better than chargin' up and down, with people stabbin' at you, ain't it?' asked Bert. 'If you wants to go, there's a sap just behind you what leads to our Lines.'

'A sap?' queried Biggles.

'Yes, sap!' said Bert. 'S-A-P—stuff what they put in trees—you know—trench, if you like. I wish I could come with you. Jerry'll be coming back in a minute, I expect. This is 'is property. We'd just driven 'im out when I copped this one in my knee and down I goes. Blighty one, I 'opes. As my missus says, "Bert," she says———'

'Hold hard!' cried Biggles. 'Let's leave what she says till another day. Can you walk?'

'With no blinkin' knee-cap?' asked Bert. 'No! And I can't 'op neither, not in this muck! What do you think I am—a sparrer?'

'No. I can see you're no sparrow,' replied Biggles, looking at the man's thirteen-stone bulk. 'And I'm no Samson to carry you, much as I should like to. I'll nip across and tell our fellows you're here. Then we'll come and fetch you.'

'You'll fetch me?' repeated Bert.

'Yes,' said Biggles.

'No sprucing?' asked the wounded man.

'What's that?' asked Biggles, with a start.

'Kiddin'. I mean, do you mean it?' explained Bert.

'Of course I mean it!' replied Biggles.

'Well, you're a toff! All right; I'll wait 'ere!'

'That's right; don't run away!' grinned Biggles. 'Where's that sap you were talking about?'

'Straight over the top, about twenty yards 'arf left,' replied Bert, pointing.

Biggles peeped stealthily over the rim of the crater. In all directions stretched a wilderness of mud and water in which barbed wire, tin helmets, rifles and ammunition-boxes lay in hopeless confusion. A bullet flipped through the ooze not an inch from his face, and he bobbed down hurriedly. But he had seen the end of the shell-shattered trench.

Turning, he looked down at Bert, whose face had turned chalky-white, and Biggles knew that in spite of his casual pose the Tommy was badly wounded, and would soon die from loss of blood if medical aid was delayed.

'Stick it, Bert, I shan't be long!' he called, dragging off his coat and throwing it to the wounded man. 'Put that over you; it'll keep you warm.' Then he darted for the end of the trench.

A fusillade of shots and the chatter of a machine-gun greeted him as, crouching low, he staggered heavily through the clinging mud. Out of the trench, as he neared it, the point of a bayonet rose to meet him, but with a shrill yell of 'Look out!' he leapt aside and then flung himself into the trench.

At the last moment he saw an infantry colonel who was talking to another officer at the end of a communication trench. He did his best to avoid them, but his foot slipped on the greasy parapet, and like a thunderbolt he struck the colonel in the small of the back. All three officers sprawled in the mud at the bottom of the trench.

The colonel was up first. Jamming a mud-coated monocle into his left eye, he glared at Biggles furiously.

'Where the dickens have you come from?' he snarled.

'My Camel landed me in this mess,' complained Biggles bitterly.

The colonel started violently.

'Camel?' he gasped. 'Have they brought up the Camel Corps?'

'That's right. That's why everyone's got the "hump"!' punned Biggles sarcastically. 'A Camel's an aeroplane in this war, not a dromedary!'

Further explanations were cut short by a shrill whistle and a cry of 'Here they come!'

'Who's coming?' cried Biggles anxiously to a burly sergeant who had sprung to the fire step and was firing his rifle rapidly.

'Father Christmas! Who do you think? 'Uns—the Prussian Guard—that's who!' snapped the N.C.O.

'Huns! Give me a rifle, someone!' pleaded Biggles.

A bomb burst somewhere near at hand, filling the trench with a thick cloud of acrid yellow smoke, and he grabbed, gasping and choking, at a rifle that leaned against the rear wall of the trench. The din of war was in his ears—the incessant rattle of rifles, the vicious crackle of machine-guns, the dull roar of heavy artillery, and the stinging crack of hand-grenades. Near at hand someone was moaning softly.

Above the noise another voice was giving orders in a crisp parade-ground voice:

'Here they come, boys—take it steady—shoot low—pick your man!'

With his head whirling, Biggles clambered up the side of the trench, still grasping his mud-coated rifle.

'Hi! Where are you going, that man? Get down, you fool!' yelled a voice.

Biggles hesitated. From the parapet he could see a long struggling line of men with fixed bayonets approaching his position at a lumbering trot. Then a hand seized his ankle and jerked him back into the trench. He swung round and found himself staring into the frowning face of the colonel, the monocle still gleaming in his eye.

'Who are you pulling about?' snarled the Camel pilot.

'What do you think you're doing?' grated the staff officer.

'I'm going to fetch Bert!' snapped Biggles.

The colonel started.

'Bert? Bert who?' he asked.

'Bert, of the Twenty-third Londons,' replied Biggles. 'He's a pal of mine, and he's out somewhere in the middle by himself.'

'In the middle?' repeated the staff officer.

'Yes!' snapped Biggles. 'In the middle of the war, he says, and I reckon he's about right!'

'You're crazy!' said the colonel. 'I can't bother about individuals—and I order you to stay where you are!'

'Order me!' stormed Biggles. 'Who do you think I am? I'm not one of your mob; I'm a flyer————'

'I don't care tuppence who you are!' replied the other. 'You're about as much good to me as a sick headache. I haven't time to argue. Another word from you, and I'll put you under close arrest for insubordination under fire!'

Biggles choked, speechless, knowing in his heart that the senior officer was well within his rights.

An orderly tumbled into the trench and handed the colonel a note. He read it swiftly, nodded, and then blew his whistle.

' "A" Company, retire! "B" Company, stand fast!' he ordered crisply. And then, turning to the sergeant: 'The Boche are in on both flanks,' he went on quickly. 'Get "A" Company back as fast as you can. "B" Company will have to cover them. And you'd better get back, too!' he snapped, turning to Biggles, who, a moment later, in spite of violent protests, found himself slipping and stumbling up a narrow, winding trench.

'But what about Bert?' he pleaded to the sergeant in front of him.

'Can't 'elp 'im. We're in the soup as it is!' snarled the N.C.O.

'The trouble about this foot-slopping game is the rotten visibility!' growled Biggles. 'It's worse than flying in clouds. No altitude, no room to move—no nothing! You blokes might call this a dog-fight, but I call it a blooming worm-fight! A lot of perishing rabbits, that's all you are, bobbing in and out of holes!'

His remarks were cut short by an explosion that filled the air with flying mud and half-buried him. He struggled to his feet, to see a white-faced orderly talking rapidly to the sergeant and pointing in rapid succession to each point of the compass.

'Surrounded, eh?' said the sergeant.

'What with?' asked Biggles breathlessly.

The sergeant eyed him scornfully.

'Mud!' he said. 'Mud and blood and 'Uns! You ought to 'ave stayed upstairs, young feller. We're in the blinking cart, and no mistake. The 'Uns are coming in on both flanks!'

'But I'm due for another patrol at six!' protested Biggles, aghast.

'You'll be patrolling the Milky Way by that time, me lad!' observed the sergeant bitterly.

Biggles turned to the orderly.

'Are you a messenger?' he said.

'I'm a runner,' replied the lad.

'Well, let's see you do a bit of running!' snapped Biggles crisply, whipping out his notebook and writing rapidly. 'You run with that,' he went on, handing the orderly a note. 'Get through the Huns somehow, and don't stop for anyone. Grab the first motor-cyclist you see, and tell him it's urgent!'

'What's the big idea?' asked the sergeant, as the runner departed at the double.

'I'm just saying goodbye to all kind friends and relations,' grinned Biggles. 'Hallo, here's old glass-house turned up again!'

The colonel, followed by a line of dishevelled, mud-coated men, staggered wearily up the communication trench.

'Line the parapets both sides!' he shouted. 'We'll get as many of them as we can before they get us! Get that gun, someone,' he snapped, pointing to a Vickers gun which, with its crew dead behind it, pointed aimlessly into the sky. 'Is there a machine-gunner here?'

'I should say so!' cried Biggles joyfully.

He dragged the gun, with its heavy tripod, clear of the mud, and mounted it on the parapet. A line of grey-clad men in coal-scuttle steel helmets was advancing stealthily up a nearby trench, and Biggles' lips parted in his famous fighting smile as he seized the spade-grips of the gun, thumbs seeking the trigger.

Rat-tat-tat-tat-tat! Rat-tat-tat-tat-tat!

The grey line wilted and sagged.

'Fill some more belts for me!' shouted Biggles, ducking as a bullet cut through the loose flap of his flying-helmet.

'Here, stick that on your head!' cried the colonel, passing him a steel helmet. 'Can you see anything?' he went on, crawling up beside him.

'I can,' replied Biggles shortly. 'Huns to the right of us, Huns to the left of us—and Huns blinking well above us! Look at that nosy parker!' he snarled, jerking his thumb upwards to where an Albatross had appeared like magic in the sky, guns spouting lead into their trench.

Biggles flung himself on his back and jerked the muzzle of his gun upwards. He knew what few infantry-men knew—the distance it is necessary to shoot in front of a rapidly-moving target in order to hit it. He aimed not at the machine, but well in front of it on its line of flight. He pressed the double thumb-piece. A stream of lead soared upwards.

The German pilot was either careless or a novice, for he did not trouble to alter his course in conditions where straight flying was almost suicidal. Straight into Biggles' line of fire he flew. The watchers in the trench saw the black-crossed machine swerve, and then, with engine roaring full on, plunge downward into the sea of mud. They could hear the crash above the noise of the battle.

'Got the blighter!' chuckled the sergeant. 'Good shooting, sir!'

'Oh, I hope he didn't land on top of poor old Bert!' gasped Biggles. 'He must have been mighty close. I can see his tail sticking up near my Camel. I wonder will that one count on my score?' he asked the colonel. 'Although I don't suppose they'll believe it, anyway.'

'I'll confirm it,' said the colonel vigorously; 'that is, if we get out alive. We're in a nasty hole!'

'So I see,' retorted Biggles, taking him literally. 'And

I don't think much of it. I'm no mole. I like doing my fighting sitting down, and where I can see what's going on.'

'I'm afraid we haven't a hope,' went on the colonel casually. 'The brigadier won't risk the brigade up here in broad daylight to get us out. We're for it, unless a miracle happens—and the day of miracles has passed.'

'Don't you be too sure about that,' returned Biggles, spraying a group of sprawling Boche with bullets. 'What about those?' he added, jerking his thumb upwards.

The colonel cocked his eye towards a little cluster of black specks that had appeared high in the blue.

'What can they do?' he asked.

'Do? You watch 'em and see!' said Biggles. 'Give me a Very pistol, so that I can fire a light to show them where we are.'

'Who are they?' asked the other.

'Friends of mine,' replied Biggles. 'I sent them word by a runner that their services were urgently required, and unless I'm very much mistaken the boys in this trench are going to see a treat for tired eyes. That's Mahoney in front—you can spot his machine a mile off. And that's Mac over on the left.'

'Oh!' he went on incredulously. 'What's all this coming behind them? A squadron of S.E.s, with old Wilks leading! The C.O. must have phoned 287 Squadron after he got my message,' he grinned, and let out a shrill whoop of triumph. 'Here, we'd better bob down a bit, or we're likely to stop something,' he went on. 'I've an idea that this locality is going to be a pretty warm spot for the next few minutes when those lads start doing their stuff. Oh—look at that!'

'That' was a line of Camels that plunged down out of the blue and scoured the ground with double lines of glittering tracer bullets. Straight along the war-torn earth they roared, guns rattling, bullets stuttering a

deadly tattoo on the ground. At the end of their dive the
Camels soared upwards to let the S.E.s go by, and then,
after a steep, stalling turn, came down again, raking the
earth with streams of lead. The colonel watched in
stupefied amazement. Biggles slid down the parapet
and caught the sergeant by the sleeve.

'Now, sergeant,' he said tersely, 'I've got you out of a
hole, and I want you to help me get someone else out of
one.'

'You bet I will!' cried the N.C.O. delightedly.

'Come on, then!' cried Biggles, darting down the
trench towards the old front line that had been their
original position.

Reaching it, he did not stop, but slithered across the
intervening stretch of mud towards the crater near the
crashed Camel. Bullets zipped and whined about them,
and Biggles had a fleeting glimpse of a grey-clad figure
rising about thirty yards in front of him, one arm raised
in the act of throwing. Instinctively he flung himself
full-length in the mud, dragging the sergeant with him.
A moment later, a roar to their left, accompanied by a
flame-hearted explosion, told them where a hand-
grenade thrown by the German had struck.

Almost before the flurry of the explosion had subsided, Biggles was on his feet again, the sergeant following
closely at his heels. Scrambling and slithering over the
ground, they made a few more paces' headway. Then
again that grey-clad figure rose up, and again the arm
swung. But this time the grenade was not thrown. From
somewhere behind them came the sharp crack of a rifle,
and the German bomb-thrower sagged in mid-air in the
very act of throwing.

It was the Britishers' chance—and they took it.
Crouching low, they sped across to the crater where
Bert was waiting, and scrambled down beside the
wounded man.

Bert was sitting just as he had left him, calmly smoking a cigarette.

'Here you are!' he cried. 'I thought you'd gone without me. When I tell my missus about this she'll say, "Bert," she'll say———'

Biggles seized him unceremoniously by the scruff of the neck.

'Take his feet, sergeant,' he panted; and together they bore the wounded man to the rear.

They found the colonel where they had left him.

'What are you up to?' he shouted, as Biggles and the sergeant came into view with their burden. 'I've been waiting for you. Couldn't make out where you'd disappeared to. The machines have opened up the communication trenches, and we can get through now. We'd better be going.'

Half an hour later, Biggles was washing the grime of war from his face in a headquarters dug-out behind the support trenches. The senior officer, monocle still in place was talking.

'It was jolly smart of you to hold up the Boche advance by conjuring up those machines,' he said.

'Boche advance? I didn't know they were advancing,' replied Biggles. 'All directions looked alike to me.'

'Then what on earth did you do it for?' cried the Colonel.

'So that I could go and fetch Bert. What else do you think? I promised him I would, so I had to,' replied Biggles, grinning broadly.

THE BOMBER

BIGGLES, cruising along the line on a dawn patrol, pressed on the rudder-bar with his left foot as his ever-searching eyes fell on a line of white archie bursts to the south-east, far over the British lines. The colour of the bursts told him at once that the shells were being fired by British guns, for German anti-aircraft gunfire was usually black. It could only mean that one or more enemy machines were in the vicinity, an event sufficiently unusual to intrigue him immensely.

'I must look into this,' was his unspoken thought as he headed his Camel along a course which would intercept the target of the rapidly-lengthening line of archie bursts.

A small, black speck, well in front of the foremost bursts, soon became visible and his curiosity increased, for the machine was of a type unknown to him. As he drew nearer a puzzled frown lined his forehead.

'I don't believe it; it can't be true,' he murmured at last, when only a few hundred yards separated him from his objective.

The anti-aircraft fire ceased when the gunners observed his presence, and Biggles closed rapidly with the other machine, which with sublime indifference continued on its way, without paying the slightest attention to him. Large Maltese crosses on the tail and fuselage left no doubt as to its nationality.

It was the largest aeroplane Biggles had ever seen. He noted two engines, one on each side of the fuselage, and raked his memory for some rumour or gossip by which he could identify it.

'It isn't a Gotha,' he mused. 'Dashed if I know what it is; but I'll bet she carries a tidy load of eggs.'

Almost unconsciously he had been edging nearer to the nose of the big machine as he inspected it, but a sudden burst of fire from the gunner in the nacelle, and an ominous *flack! flack! flack!* behind warned him that the crew were on the alert and well prepared to receive him. He made a lightning right-hand turn, and as he flashed back past the bomber a murderously accurate burst of fire from the rear gunner startled him still further.

'Strewth!' swore Biggles. 'This is a bit hot.'

The big machine had not moved an inch from its course, and to be thus treated with contempt annoyed him intensely. They were rapidly approaching the Lines and if he was to prevent the return of the bomber to its aerodrome, something would have to be done quickly.

Biggles swept to the rear of the machine, muttering again as the Camel bumped violently in the slipstream of the two engines.

'All right, let's see how you like this one,' he snapped angrily, and put his nose down in a steep dive. He was following the usual practice of attacking a two-seater, judging his speed and distance to bring him up under the elevators of the enemy machine, out of the field of fire of both gunners.

The attack was perfectly timed and the Camel soared up like a bird immediately under the big fuselage. Biggles glanced through the sights and took the bomber at where he judged the pilot's seat to be, withholding his fire until the Camel was almost at stalling point in order to make certain of his aim. What happened next occurred with startling rapidity. The muzzles of a pair of twin Parabellum guns slid out of a trap-door in the floor of the bomber and the next instant a double stream of lead was shooting the Camel to pieces about him. *Flack! Flack! Whang! Whang!* sang the bullets as they bored through fabric and metal. Biggles, shaken as never before in all his flying experience, kicked out his left foot spasmodically and flung the stick over and back into his stomach. The Camel whirled over and fell into a dive; the 150 h.p. Bentley Rotary coughed once—twice—and then cut out altogether. The propeller stopped dead and the thoroughly alarmed pilot started to glide earthwards with the rapidly-diminishing hum of the bomber's engines in his ears.

Biggles pushed up his goggles and looked downwards, and then up at the fast disappearing Boche machine.

'Phew!' he breathed soberly. 'That'll stop me laughing in church in the future. What a trap. Who would have guessed it? Well, we live and learn,' he concluded bitterly, and turned his attention to the inevitable forced landing. He anticipated no difficulty, for he had ample height from which to choose a landing ground. 'Thank goodness I'm over my own side of the line,' he mused philosophically, as he slowly lost height.

He could not get to his own aerodrome, at Maranique, but 287 Squadron might just be reached, and although he did not look forward with any degree of pleasure to the inevitable jibes of the S.E.5 pilots it was better than risking damaging the machine in an open field.

He made a good landing in the middle of the aerodrome and sat up on the 'hump' of the Camel to await the arrival of the mechanics to tow the machine to the tarmac, where a group of cheering pilots awaited him.

'Get stung, Biggles?' yelled Wilkinson, the good-natured flight-commander.

'I got stung all right,' acknowledged Biggles ruefully. 'That kite's got more stings than a hornet's nest. What is it, anyway?'

'That's our pet Friedrichshafen. Come and have a drink while we ring up your old man and tell him you're O.K., and I'll tell you about it,' said Wilks, linking his arm through that of the Camel pilot's.

'Have you had a go at it?' inquired Biggles.

'Me? We've all had a go at it. It comes over just before dawn nearly every day, lays its eggs, and beetles home about this time.'

'And so you mean to say that you can't stop it?' exclaimed Biggles incredulously.

Wilkinson shrugged his shoulders. 'You didn't do a lot yourself, did you? The only thing that did any stopping was your cowling, by the look of it. It's as full of holes as a colander. It'd be easier to sink a battleship than that flying arsenal. There isn't a blind spot anywhere that we've discovered; the usual weak spots aren't weak any longer. They just plaster you whichever way you come—oh! I know. Twin mobile guns'll beat fixed guns any day. I'm not aching to commit suicide, so I let it alone, and that's a fact. There was a rumour that Wing had offered three pips to anybody who got it. Lacie of 281 had a go, and went down in flames. Crickson of 383 had a stab at it in one of the new Dolphins, and it took a week to dig him out of the ground. Most people keep their distance now and watch archie do its stuff; but *they* couldn't hit a Zeppelin at fifty yards. Guns[1] reckons that the Friedrichshafen costs our people, who are paying for the War, five thousand pounds a day for archie ammunition, and I reckon he isn't far out.'

'I see,' said Biggles thoughtfully. 'Well, I'll be getting back if you can find me transport. I'll come back for the Camel later on. Cheerio, Wilks.'

'Cheerio, Biggles. Keep away from that Hun till the first of the month. I'll send you a wreath, but I'm broke till then.'

[1] *'Guns' was the usual squadron nickname for the gunnery officer.*

'Yes? Well, don't chuck your money away on losers. What you'll need is a pair of spectacles next time I meet that Hun.'

After seeing the damaged Camel brought home, and the ignition lead which had caused the engine failure repaired, Biggles spent the evening with a lead pencil and some paper, making drawings of the big bomber as he remembered it. He marked the three guns and drew lines and circles to represent the field of fire covered by each. He quickly discovered that what Wilkinson had told him concerning the guns covering all angles of approach was correct, and ordinary attack was almost useless, and certainly very dangerous.

The old weakness in the defence of all big machines, which was underneath the fuselage, did not exist. The only possible spot which could be regarded as 'blind' was immediately under the nacelle, and even so he would be exposed to the fire of at least one of the gunners while he was manoeuvring into that position. He considered the possibility of dropping bombs, but discarded it as impracticable. If he dropped the bombs over his own side of the line and missed, the people down below would have something to say about it, and it was hardly likely that he would be allowed to go about it unmolested over the German side.

No! The only chance was the spot under the nacelle and then use a Lewis gun which fired upwards through his centre section. He did not usually carry this weapon, and he infinitely preferred head-on tactics with his double Vickers guns. Not entirely satisfied with the result of his calculations, he gave instructions for the Lewis gun to be fitted, told his batman to call him an hour before dawn, and went to bed.

It was still dark when, with his flying coat and boots over his pyjamas, he climbed into the cockpit of his

Camel the following morning. He felt desperately tired and disinterested in the project, and half regretted his decision to pursue it, but once in the air he felt better.

It was a glorious morning. A few late stars still lingered in the sky; to the east the first gleam of dawn was lightening the horizon. He pointed his nose and cruised steadily in the direction of his encounter of the preceding day, climbing steadily and inhaling the fresh morning air. As he climbed, the rim of the sun, still visible to those below, crept up over the skyline and bathed the Camel in an orange glow. Around and below him the earth was a vast basin of indigo and deep purple shadows, stretching, it seemed, to eternity. He appeared to hang over the centre of it, an infinitesimal speck in a strange world in which no other living creature moved. The sense of utter loneliness and desolation, well known to pilots, oppressed him, and he was glad when six D.H.9s, which had crept up unseen from the void beneath, gleamed suddenly near him like jewels on velvet as the rays of the sun flashed on their varnished wings. He flew closer to them and waved to the observers leaning idly over their Scarff rings.[1] The Nines held on their way and were soon lost in the mysterious distance. Biggles idly wondered how many of them would come back. The dome above him had turned pale-green, and then turquoise, not slowly, but quickly, as if hidden lights had been switched on by the master of a stage performance.

'And this is war!' mused the pilot. 'It's hard to believe—but unless I'm mistaken here it comes,' he added, as his eye caught a cluster of tiny sparks in the far distance at about his own height. 'Good morning, Archibald, you dirty dog,' he muttered, as he eyed the approaching flashes, at the head of which he could now discern the silhouette of the big bomber. He swiftly closed the distance between them, warming his guns as

[1] *Gun-mountings.*

he went, and the answering stream of tracer from the forward guns of the bomber brought a faint smile to his lips. There was no chance of approaching unobserved and he had not attempted it. He circled slowly 500 feet above the big machine and looked down; the gunner in the rear cockpit gave him a mock salute, and waved back.

He wasted no further time on pleasantries, but dived steeply, still well outside effective range. Down and down he went until he was well below the bomber and then slowly pulled the stick back; the bomber seemed to be dropping out of the sky on to him. He was coming up under the nacelle and his eyes were glued to the trap-door, through which he could see the crouching gunner. A spurt of flame leapt outwards towards him and the ominous tell-tale *flack! flack!* behind and on each side told that the gunner was making good shooting. A moment later he was flying on even keel not more than twenty feet below the nacelle and in the same direction as the other machine.

Something seemed to drop off the bomber and whizz past him; he looked upwards with a start, in time to see another bomb swing off the bomb-rack and hurtle past dangerously near. He looked along the line of racks, but could see no more bombs, which relieved him greatly, for he had entirely overlooked the fact that the bomber might not have laid all its eggs. He could see the face of the forward gunner peering over the side, looking at him, and a quick glance astern revealed spasmodic bursts of tracer passing harmlessly under the tail of the Camel. Satisfied that the gunner could not reach him, he took the joystick between his knees and seized his top gun, left hand grasping the spade grip and right fore-finger curled around the trigger. *Rat-tat*—— He muttered as he struggled to clear the jammed gun. Why did guns always jam at the crucial moment?

The bomber was turning now and he had to grab the stick with one hand to keep his place. He stood up in the cockpit and hammered at the ammunition drum with his fist. He tried the trigger, found the gun was working and dropping back into his seat, just had time to push the stick forward as the bomber came down on him as its pilot tried to tear his wing off with its under-carriage. He side-slipped in a wild attempt to keep in position, but his windscreen flew to pieces as a stream of tracer from the rear gun caught him. He dived frantically away, kicking alternate feet as he went to spoil the gunner's aim.

Safely out of range, he pushed up his goggles and wiped his forehead. 'Dash this for a game,' he moaned, 'but for that jam I'd have had him then.'

He glanced down and was horrified to see that they were already over the enemy's lines. He tested his top gun to make sure that it was working and then savagely repeated his manoeuvre to come up underneath the bomber. He held his breath as he ran the gauntlet of the gunners again, and then at point-blank range he dropped the stick, seized the gun and pressed the trigger.

There was no mistake this time. He held the burst until the Camel began to fall away from under him and then he dropped back into his seat, grabbing wildly at the stick as the machine went into a spin, bracing himself with all his strength against the sides of the cockpit to prevent himself being thrown out.

'By gosh! That's all I want of that,' he muttered, as he got the machine under control and looked around for the bomber.

It was steering an erratic course for the ground, obviously in difficulties. He dived after it and noticed that the rear gunner's cockpit was empty.

'I've hit the pilot, and the observer is trying to get the

machine down,' he decided instantly, and a closer view confirmed his suspicions, for he could see the observer holding the joystick over the shoulder of the limp figure of the pilot. 'I hope he manages it,' thought Biggles anxiously, and held his hand up to show that they had nothing more to fear from him, afterwards circling round to watch the landing. It was a creditable effort; the big machine flattened out, but failed to clear a line of trees; Biggles almost fancied he could hear the crash as it settled down in a pile of torn fabric and splintered wood.

'I'll have to go and tell Wilks about this,' said Biggles to himself, as he steered a course for the S.E.5 aerodrome. 'He'll be tickled to death!'

ON LEAVE

BIGGLES, glanced up carelessly at the noticeboard in passing; a name caught his eye and he took a step nearer. The name was his own. He read:

Captain J.C. Bigglesworth: posted to 69 F.T.S. Narborough. W./48 P./1321.

For a full minute he looked at the notice uncomprehendingly, and as its full significance dawned upon him strode purposefully to the Squadron office.

'Yes, Biggles?' said Major Mullen, glancing up from his desk. 'Do you want to see me?'

'I see I'm posted to Home Establishment,' replied Biggles. 'May I ask why?'

The C.O. laid down his pen, crossed the room and laid a fatherly hand on the flight-commander's shoulder. 'I'm sorry, Biggles,' he said simply, 'but I've got to send you home. Now listen to me. I've been out here longer than you have. I know every move in the game; that's why I'm commanding 266. I know when a man's cracking up; I saw you start weeks ago; when Batson went west you were at breaking-point. Now, remember, I'm telling you this is for your own good—not to hurt your feelings. I think too much of you for that. If I thought less of you, why, I'd leave you here to go on piling up the score in the Squadron "game book". If you did stay here, you wouldn't last a month. You'll be caught napping; you'll stall taking-off, or you'll hit a tree coming in. Cleverer pilots than you have gone out that way. You can't help it and you can't stop it. No one can stand the pace for ever. This game makes an old man of a young one without him knowing it. That's the truth, Biggles. You've got to have a rest. If you don't rest now you'll never be able to rest again. You are more use to us alive than dead; put it that way if you like. That's why I put your posting through.'

'But can't I have a rest without being posted?' said Biggles bitterly.

'No; I have asked you to take some leave. The M.O. has asked you, and I've heard Mac and Mahoney telling you to—they've both been on leave and it's done them a power of good.'

'All right, sir. I'll go on leave if you'll cancel the posting. It would kill me to hang about an F.T.S.[1]'

'Very well. Fill in your application. Ten days, with effect from tomorrow. I'll send it to Wing by hand right away. You stay on the strength of 266.'

'I've only one other thing to ask, sir. May I fly home?'

'There you go, you see. You can't leave it alone. Well, you might get a lift with a ferry pilot from Bourget. How's that?'

'Not for me,' said Biggles firmly. 'I'm not trusting my life to any ferry pilot. I'll fly myself in a Camel.'

'How am I going to account for the Camel if you break it up?'

'Break it up! I don't break machines up.'

'You might.'

'Well, send one back for reconditioning. I'll take it.'

'All right,' said the C.O. after a brief pause. 'It's against regulations and you know it. Don't come back here without that Camel, that's all.'

'Very good, sir.'

Biggles saluted briskly and departed.

Major Mullen turned to 'Wat' Tyler, the Recording Officer, who had been a witness to the scene, and deliberately winked. 'You were right, Tyler,' he smiled. 'That posting worked the trick; that was the only way we would have got him to take some leave.'

[1] *Flying Training School.*

Early the following morning Biggles, in his best uniform, took off and steered a course for Marquise, where he proposed to refuel before crossing the Channel. He eyed the enemy sky longingly, but true to his word to the C.O. held firmly to his way. The trip proved uneventful, and midday found him lunching in the officers' mess at Lympne. He reported to the officer commanding the station, presenting his movement order, saw his machine safely in a hangar, and went on to London by train. Arriving home, he discovered the house closed; he telephoned a friend of the family, only to find out that his father and brother, his only living relations, were in the Army and 'somewhere in France'.

'Well, that's that,' said Biggles, as he hung up the receiver. 'I might have known they would be.'

For a week he hung about town, thoroughly bored, doing little except drift between his hotel and anywhere he thought he might strike somebody he knew, home on leave from the Front. The weather was cold and wet and he looked forward joyfully to his return to the Squadron. And then, walking down Shaftesbury Avenue, he met Dick Harboard, his father's greatest friend and business associate. Over some coffee Biggles briefly explained his position, bitterly lamenting the time he was wasting when he might be doing something useful in France.

'I'm sick of loafing about here,' he concluded. 'London is getting me down fast. I hate the sight of the place, but there's nowhere else to go.'

'Why not come down to my place for the rest of your time. I've a shooting party down for the week-end. Mixed crowd, of course—some funny people have got the money these days—but it can't be helped. What about it?'

'Where is your place.'

'Felgate, in Kent—near Folkestone.'

'Folkestone is near Lympne, isn't it?'

'Next door to it. Why?'

'Oh, I just wondered,' said Biggles vaguely. He did not think it worth while explaining that he had a machine at Lympne and had visions of putting in a few hours' flying-time if the weather improved.

'Good enough,' said Harboard as they parted. 'I shall expect you tonight in time for dinner.'

'I'll be along,' agreed Biggles. 'I'll come down in mufti, I think, and forget the war for a bit. Cheerio—see you later.'

Biggles, clad in grey flannels and a sweater, deep in a novel from his host's library, paused to pull his chair a little nearer to the hall fire. It was bitterly cold for the time of the year; lowering skies and a drizzle of rain had put all idea of flying out of his head, and he settled down for a comfortable spell of reading.

He frowned as the door opened to admit a party of men and girls whose heavy boots and mackintoshes proclaimed them to be a shooting party, bound for the fields. At their head was Frazer, a big, florid, middle-aged man to whom Biggles had taken an instant dislike when they had been introduced the previous evening. Biggles did not like the easy air of familiarity with which he had addressed him. His loud, overbearing manner, particularly when there were women present, irritated his frayed nerves. He had noticed on arrival that none of the party was in uniform, and he wondered vaguely why a man of such obviously splendid physique as Frazer was not in the Army; to save any possible embarrassment he had asked to be introduced as Mr. Bigglesworth. He was not left long in wonder, for Frazer, tapping his chest ruefully with his forefinger, complained at frequent intervals of the weak heart that kept him at home and thus prevented him from showing in actual practice how the war could be ended forth-

with. The fact that he was obviously making a lot of
money out of the war did nothing to lessen Biggles'
irritation, and these were the reasons why he had decided to remain in the hall with a book rather than have
to suffer the fellow's society with the shooting party.

'Well, well,' observed Frazer in affected surprise,
with his eyes on the slippers on Biggles' feet. 'Not
coming out with the guns?'

'No, thanks,' replied Biggles civilly.

'Huh! I should have thought a bit of exercise would
have done you good; a shot or two at the birds will get
your eye in for when you join the Army.' The sneer
behind the words was unmistakable.

'It's too confoundedly cold, and I hate getting my feet
wet,' said Biggles quietly, keeping his temper with an
effort.

'I can't understand you young fellows,' went on
Frazer, when the snigger that had followed Biggles'
words had subsided. 'Anyway, I should have thought
there were plenty of things you could do with a war on
besides rotting over a fire.'

Again the inference was obvious, and Biggles choked
back a hot retort. 'Bah! Why argue,' was his unspoken
thought. The man was in his element, holding the floor;
well, let him. He eyed Frazer coldly, without answering,
and it may have been something in his eye that caused
Frazer to shift uneasily and turn to the outside door.

'Well, let's get along, folks,' he said loudly. 'Somebody has got to keep the home fires burning, I suppose,'
was his parting shot as the door closed behind them.

Biggles, left alone, smiled to himself for a moment,
and then settled down to his book. The telephone in the
next room shrilled noisily—again, and yet again, and
Biggles breathed a prayer of thankfulness when he
heard Lea, the butler, answer it. He was half-way
through the first chapter of his book when the phone

again jarred his nerves with its insistent jangle. He laid down his book with a weary sigh. 'My gosh! I can't stand this infernal racket,' he muttered, and looked up to see Lea standing white-faced in the doorway.

'What's the matter, Lea?' he asked irritably. 'Is the house on fire or something?'

'No, sir; but Mr. Harboard is out. He is the chief Constable, you know, and they say that two German seaplanes are bombing Ramsgate.'

'What?' Biggles leapt up as if he had been stung by a hornet. 'Say that again.'

'Two German seaplanes————'

Biggles made a flying leap to the window and cast a critical eye at the sky. The rain had stopped and small patches of blue showed through the scudding clouds.

'Quick!' he snapped, every nerve tingling with excitement. 'Get the car round.'

The butler, shaken from his normal sedate bearing by the brisk command, departed almost at a run.

'Get me to Lympne as quickly as you can; put your foot down and keep it down,' Biggles told the chauffeur a few minutes later, as, with flying-coat, cap and goggles over his arm, he jumped into the big saloon car.

For fifteen minutes Biggles fretted and fumed with impatience as the car tore through the narrow Kentish lanes.

'Go on,' he shouted, when they arrived at the aerodrome, 'straight up to the hangar.'

The guard at the gate challenged him, but Biggles yelled him aside with a swift invective.

'Get that Camel out of No. 3 shed,' he snapped at a group of idling mechanics. 'Number 9471—jump to it!' and then he burst into the C.O.'s office.

'Captain Bigglesworth, 266 Squadron, on leave from overseas, sir. You remember I reported last week?'

'Oh, yes, I remember,' said the C.O. 'What's the hurry?'

'Two Huns are bombing Ramsgate—I'm going for them. I've got ammunition—and I had two belts put in in case I ran into anything coming over.'

'But———'

Biggles was already on his way; he took a flying leap into the cockpit.

'Switches off, petrol on,' sang out the ack-emma.

'Petrol on,' echoed Biggles.

'Contact!'

'Contact!'

The Bentley started with a roar and sent a cloud of smoke whirling aft in the slipstream. He adjusted his goggles, waved the chocks away, and a few minutes later was in the air heading N.N.W., with the coastline cutting across the leading edge of his starboard wing. He had no maps, but he estimated the distance to Ramsgate to be about fifteen to twenty miles, not more; with the wind under his tail he should be there in less than ten minutes. Deal was on his starboard quarter now, and Sandwich loomed ahead; in the distance he could see the sweep in the coast where the North Foreland jutted out.

He had been flying low in order to watch the landmarks, but now he pulled the joystick back and climbed through a convenient hole in the clouds. Above, the cloud-tops were bathed in brilliant sunshine, and, still climbing, he looked eagerly ahead for the enemy machines. The only machine he could see was an old F.E. circling aimlessly some distance inland, so he pointed his nose north-west and headed out to sea in an endeavour to cut the raiders off should they have started on the homeward journey.

For a quarter of an hour he flew thus, peering ahead and around him for the hostile machines. Doubts began to assail him. Suppose the whole thing was a wild rumour? What a fool he had been not to get some reliable information before he started. His altimeter was registering 10,000 feet; the clouds through which he could occasionally see patches of grey sea, were far below.

He commenced a wide circle back towards land, noting that he had already ventured much too far away to be safe should his engine give trouble. He throttled back to three-quarters and for a few minutes cruised quietly in a due easterly direction, touching his rudder-bar from time to time to permit a clear view ahead.

A movement—or was it instinct—made him glance to the north. Far away, flying close together, were two machines—seaplanes. He was round in an instant heading north-west to cut them off. Five minutes later he could see that he would catch them, for they were appreciably nearer. He could tell the moment they saw him, for they turned in a more northerly direction away from him and put their noses down for more speed. A few minutes later he could see the black crosses and the gunners standing up waiting to receive him.

'Well,' mused Biggles, 'this is no place to mess about in a Camel. If I run out of fuel, or if they get a shot in my tank, I'm sunk. I must have been crazy to come right out here. It's neck or nothing if I'm going to do anything. Here goes.'

He pushed his nose down for speed and then pulled up in a steep zoom under the elevators of the nearest machine; but the pilot had seen his move and swung broadside on and exposed him to the full view of his gunner, who at once opened fire; but his shooting was wild, and Biggles could see his tracer passing harmlessly some distance away. The Camel pilot deliberately hung back until the other had emptied his drum of ammunition and started to replace it with a new one;

then he zoomed in to point-blank range, and, knowing that he might not get such another opening, held his fire until his sights were aligned on the forward cockpit, and then pressed his triggers.

The nose of the Brandenburg seaplane tilted sharply upwards, and then dropped; the machine made an aimless half-turn that quickly became a spin as the nose dropped, and then whirled downwards with the engine still at full throttle.

Biggles fell off on to his wing and peered through his centre section for the second seaplane. For a moment he could not see it, and when he did spot it it was going down in a steep dive towards the clouds.

'Looks as if he's lost his nerve,' muttered the Camel pilot, as he pushed his stick forward and went down like a thunderbolt in the wake of the diving German.

He opened fire some distance away at a range which he knew quite well could not be effective unless a lucky shot found its mark, but he did it with the deliberate intention of rattling an obviously nervous foe.

The Brandenburg dropped tail-up into the cloud-bank and Biggles carefully followed it; he found it again just below the clouds and resumed the chase. Just ahead, a wide patch of blue sky showed through a gap in the cloud, and Biggles closed in quickly, but the German swung round in obvious indecision.

'The fool can't be thinking of trying to land,' thought Biggles in astonishment, and fired a series of short bursts to confuse his opponent still more.

But the German had had enough, and apparently having no wish to share the fate of his companion, cut off his engine and commenced to glide down towards the water.

A new possibility occurred to Biggles. 'If he gets that kite down on the water safely the gunner might be able to hold me off.' A floating target would be more difficult to hit than one in the air, for he dare not risk overshooting his mark. 'Well, I've got to cramp his style,' thought Biggles, and he dived recklessly at the seaplane, guns streaming tracer, to which, to his surprise, the enemy gunner made no reply. 'What a gutless hound,' he thought. 'Hullo—there he goes!'

The Brandenburg pilot, in his haste to get out of that withering blast of lead, had tried to land too fast; the floats struck the surface of the sea with a terrific splash; the nose buried itself under the water and the tail cocked high into the air. Biggles watched both occupants climb along the elevators, and, circling low, pointed in the direction of the shore, in the hope that they would realize that he had gone for help.

'You are wanted on the phone, sir,' said Lea, the butler, apologetically.

It was late in the afternoon. Biggles put down his book and hurried to the instrument, for he was expecting the call, and anxious to hear the fate of the two German airmen. He picked up the receiver.

'Major Sidgrove speaking, from Lympne,' said a voice.

'Captain Bigglesworth here, sir,' replied Biggles.

'Good show, Bigglesworth; we found both machines in the sea. The crew of the first were both dead—gunshot wounds—but the others were all right except for shock and exposure. Rather funny; the pilot had a brace of beautiful black eyes that the observer had given him. The pilot was an N.C.O. under the command of an officer in the rear seat; the Germans fly like that, you know.'

Biggles knew well enough, but he made no comment.

'Apparently it was the pilot's first show,' went on the Major, 'and when you started shooting he went to bits. He made for the water with the officer beating hell out of him and yelling for him to get into the clouds. He was swiping him over the nut instead of shooting at you. I've never seen a man so peeved in my life. Well, that's all. I thought you'd like to know. I've forwarded your report to the Ministry. They've been on the phone wanting to know what the dickens you were doing at Lympne, where you got the Camel, who gave you instructions, and goodness knows what else! They seem more concerned about that than about the two Huns—they would be! I expect they'll send for you during the next day or two; where can I get hold of you if they do?'

'Maranique,' replied Biggles shortly. 'I'm going back tomorrow. Many thanks, Major; goodbye.'

Biggles hung up the receiver and returned to the hall. The door opened and the shooting party, covered with mud, entered. Frazer looked at Biggles in undisguised disgust.

'Still keeping the fire warm,' he sneered. 'You should have been with us; we've had great sport.'

'So have I,' said Biggles softly.

'I got in some pretty shooting,' continued Frazer.

'Funny; so did I,' said Biggles, smiling faintly.

'You! Why, you haven't been out. I can't understand why some people are so careful about their skins.'

One of the girls came forward.

'There,' she said. 'I've brought you a little souvenir.' She laid a small white feather on the table.

'Thanks,' said Biggles evenly. 'I've always wanted a feather in my cap. I've got one today.'

Mr. Harboard bustled into the room.

'What's that—what's that—feather in your cap? I should say it will be. I shouldn't be surprised if you got the D.S.O. Well done, my boy; you deserve it.'

'D.S.O.—D.S.O.———?' echoed Frazer stupidly. 'What the devil for?'

'Haven't you heard?'

'Oh, cut it out, sir,' protested Biggles.

'Cut it out, be blowed. I'm proud to have you under my roof and I want everybody to know it.' He turned to the others. 'He's just shot down a couple of Hun bombers in the sea, after they bombed Ramsgate.'

A silence fell that could almost be felt.

'Who—who is he?' blurted out Frazer, at last, nodding towards Biggles, who was lighting a cigarette. 'He's not *the* Bigglesworth—the fellow we read about in the papers—the flyer—is he?'

'Of course he is; who else did you think he was?' cried Harboard in astonishment.

'Well,' said Frazer quietly, 'I'll be getting along. I've just had a phone call calling me up to Newcastle in the morning. I'll have to start tonight to catch my train.'

'That's all right,' said Biggles cheerfully. 'Stay the night and I'll fly you up in the morning. I can get a Bristol from Lympne.'

'No, thanks,' cried Frazer firmly.

'I can't understand some people,' said Biggles softly, as he turned towards the library, 'being so careful about their skins.'

FOG!

FOG, mist, and still more mist. Biggles crouched lower in his cockpit as the white vapour swirled aft, and wished he had taken Major Sidgrove's advice and waited at Lympne until it had lifted.

'It will clear as the sun comes up,' he had told the Major, optimistically, as he took off.

He was anxious to get back to the Squadron, and although visibility on the ground had not been good he did not think it was so bad as it proved to be in the air. At 500 feet the ground was completely hidden from view, but a glance at the compass told him that he was heading towards the French coast.

'What a day!' he muttered, and climbed steadily to get above the opaque curtain. At 5,000 feet the mist began to thin and the sun showed wanly as a pale white orb; when his altimeter told him that he was 6,000 feet above the earth, he emerged into clear sunshine with a suddenness that was startling.

'I've a poor chance of finding the aerodrome if this stuff doesn't lift,' he told himself as he skimmed along just above the pea-soup vapour.

For an hour he followed his course, peering below anxiously for a break in the mist to show him his where-abouts, but in vain.

'Well, I'd better go down and see where I am,' he muttered. He throttled back and slid once more into the bank of clammy moisture. He was flying blind now, hoping against hope that the mist would thin out before he reached the ground; if it didn't, well, he would probably crash, that's all there was to it; but sooner or

later he would have to come down, and he preferred to
do it now rather than when he was getting short of fuel.

He kept a watchful eye on the altimeter. 2,000—
1,000—500——— 'I'll be into the carpet in a minute,'
was his unspoken thought.

He went into a shallow glide, peering below anxiously, praying that his altimeter was functioning properly
and that he would not crash into a church tower or a
tree. Something dark loomed below and for a minute he
could not make out what it was.

'Strewth! It's the sea!' he ejaculated, and thrusting
the throttle wide open he began climbing swiftly. For a
moment the discovery left him stunned. 'Where the
deuce have I got to?' he said to himself, half in anger
and half in fright; 'I ought to have crossed the coast half
an hour ago. This compass is all wrong, I expect.'

He climbed above the mist and for another fifteen
minutes flew south and then dropped down again.
Something dark reared up in front of him and he
zoomed swiftly to avoid hitting a tree, but an exclama-
tion of relief escaped his lips as he saw that he was, at
least, over terra firma.

'What a day!' he muttered again, and once more
climbed up above the swirling fog, realizing that if
conditions did not improve he would be lucky to get
down without damaging the machine and possibly himself. In all directions the fog stretched in an unbroken
sea of glistening white. 'This is no use,' he mused; 'I'd
better find out where I am—it might as well be now as
later on.'

He throttled back once more and commenced
another slow glide towards the ground. At 500 feet he
could just see what appeared to be open fields below.
He S-turned, almost at stalling point, keenly alert for
any possible obstruction. When he was satisfied that all
was clear he tipped up his wing and side-slipped down;

he levelled out, switched off the ignition, and a moment later ran to a standstill not ten yards from a thick hedge. For a few moments he sat contemplating his predicament, and then climbed slowly out of the cockpit.'

'I suppose all I can do is to walk until I find a house or somebody who can tell me where I am,' he reflected ruefully, as, pushing up his goggles and loosening his throat-strap, he set off at a steady pace across the field. He was glad of his short, leather coat, for the ground-mist was cold and clammy. A hedge loomed up in front of him and he faced it blankly. 'Which way now?' he asked of himself. He thrust his hand in his trouser-pocket and pulled out a coin. 'Heads left, tails right,' he muttered. 'Heads, eh? Left it is, then'; and he once more set off parallel with the hedge. A hundred yards and another hedge appeared dimly in front of him. 'Let's have a look what's over the other side,' he muttered, as he took a flying leap and landed on top of it. A sunken road, or, rather, a cart-track, lay before him. 'I wish this infernal mist would clear,' he thought petulantly, as he set off down the road. 'Hullo! Here's signs of life, anyway.' On his right was a row of poles which reminded him of the hop-fields he had often seen in Kent; a thick layer of greenery was spread over the tops of the wires that connected them. 'Don't tell me I'm back home again,' he said, aghast. 'No, by thunder; it's camouflage!' He paused in his stride to survey what was the finest and certainly the largest piece of camouflage he had ever seen. Below it the ground fell away suddenly into a steep dip, and across the intervening valley stretched row after row of posts, criss-crossed at the top with wires, and the whole covered with a layer of drab green canvas and imitation grass.

'Whew!' he whistled. 'Whatever's under that would take a bit of spotting from the air.' He bent down and peered below the concealing canopy, but could only see what appeared to be a number of grey cisterns and cylinders. 'Beats me,' he muttered, as he continued his walk. 'Well, here's someone coming, anyway, so we'll soon know.'

On the left a gate opened into the field he had just left, and he leaned against it carelessly, awaiting the arrival of the owners of the approaching footsteps.

'It sounds like troops,' was his unspoken thought as he lit a cigarette and gazed pensively into the grey mist that hung like a blanket over the field.

The footsteps of marching men were close now, and he turned casually in their direction. The sight that met his eyes seemed to freeze his heart into a block of ice. The shock was so great that he did not move, but stood rigid as if he had been transformed into a block of granite. Out of the mist, not ten yards away, straight down the middle of the road, marched a squad of grey steel-helmeted German soldiers, an N.C.O. at their head.

Biggles looked at them with a face of stone, praying that they would not hear the tumultuous beating of his heart. There was a sharp word of command; as in a dream he saw the N.C.O.'s hand go up in salute, and his return of the salute was purely automatic. Another word of command and the troops had disappeared into the mist.

For a full minute Biggles gazed after them, utterly and completely stunned, and then a thousand thoughts flooded into his brain at once. Nauseating panic seized him, and he ran to and fro in agitated uncertainty. Never before had he experienced anything like the sensation of helplessness that possessed him now.

'Steady, steady, you fool!' he snarled, as he fought to get a grip on himself. 'Think—think!'

Sanity returned at last and he listened intently. In the distance someone was hammering metal against metal. *Clang! Clang! Clang!* boomed the sound dully through the enveloping mist.

They took me for one of their own pilots—of course they would. Why should they expect a British pilot to be standing gaping at them? Thank goodness I had my coat on, were thoughts that rushed through his mind.

A little farther down the road a large notice faced him, and he wondered how he had failed to see it before.

ACHTUNG! LEBENSGEFAHR

CHLORGASANSTALT

EINTRITT STRENG VERBOTEN

Chlorgasanstalt! Gas! In an instant he understood everything; the camouflage covered a Hun gas-manufacturing plant.

'I'll be getting out of this,' he muttered, and, vaulting over the gate, set off at a run across the field in the direction of the Camel. Another hedge faced him; he struggled through it and found himself in a field of roots. 'This isn't it,' he muttered hoarsely, and realised with horror that he had lost his sense of direction. He clambered back into the field he had just left and raced down the side of the hedge, pulling up with a cry of despair as the edge of the wood suddenly faced him.

He knew he was lost. 'Curse this fog; where am I?' he groaned out viciously. It was suddenly lighter and he glanced upwards; the mist was lifting at last, slowly, but already he could see the silvery disc of the sun. 'The Boche'll see the Camel as soon as I shall,' he pondered, hopelessly, 'and the farther I go now the farther I shall get away from it. If they spot it, I'm sunk.'

Another thought occurred to him—what of his discovery? Quite apart from saving his own skin he was now in possession of information which the Headquarters Staff would willingly give fifty officers to possess—the whereabouts of the German gas supply dump.

'If I do get away I can't tell them where it is,' he mused; 'I don't know where I am to within a hundred miles. Dash that compass!'

He started; someone was coming towards him. He dived into the undergrowth and crouched low, scarcely daring to breathe. The newcomer was a Belgian peasant, garbed in the typical garments of a worker on the land; in his hand he carried a hedger's hook. He was a filthy specimen of his class, dirty and unshaven, and Biggles watched him anxiously as he plodded along muttering to himself, glancing from time to time to left and right.

'I wonder if I dare risk speaking—if he would help me?' thought Biggles.

But the risk was too great and he dismissed the idea from his mind. The peasant was opposite him now, snivelling and wiping his nose on the back of his hand. He stopped suddenly and listened intently.

'Where are you?'

The words, spoken in English in a quick sibilant hiss from somewhere near at hand, stunned Biggles into a frozen state of immobility for the second time within a quarter of an hour. His heart seemed to stop beating and he felt the blood drain from his face. Who had spoken? Had anybody spoken—or had he imagined it? Were his nerves giving out? He didn't know, but he bit his lip to prevent himself crying out.

'Where are you?'

Again came the words in a low penetrating whisper, but in an educated English voice.

'Here,' said Biggles involuntarily.

The peasant swung round on his heel and hurried towards him. 'Your machine is in the next field,' he said quickly; 'hurry up, you've no time to lose. Fifty yards—look out—get down!'

Biggles flung himself back into the undergrowth and

pressed himself into the bottom of the ditch that skirted the wood. The peasant's hook flashed above him and a tangle of briars covered him. Through them Biggles could just see the Belgian lopping at the hedge unconcernedly, muttering to himself as he did so. Guttural voices jarred the silence somewhere near at hand and a group of German soldiers, carrying mess tins, loomed into his field of vision. Without so much as a glance at the hedge-trimmer they passed on and were swallowed up in the mist.

'Quick now,' said the voice again; 'run for it. There's an archie battery fifty yards down there—you were walking straight into it; I saw you land, and I've been chasing you ever since.'

'What about the gasworks?' said Biggles irrelevantly.

The pseudo-Belgian started violently. 'What gasworks?' he said, in a curiously strained voice.

'The Hun gas dump,' replied Biggles.

'Where is it?'

'Just across there at the corner of the wood; it's well camouflaged.'

'Great heaven! You've stumbled on the thing I've been looking for for three weeks. Get back and report it in case I am taken before I can loose a carrier pigeon. Here comes the sun—turn right down the hedge, fifty yards, then get through the hedge and you will see the machine in front of you.'

'Where am I now?' inquired Biggles.

'Thirty kilos north-west of Courtrai—one mile due east of Berslaade.'

'Aren't you coming? I can take you on the wing.'

'No; I'll stay here and see what damage the bombers do.'

'What's your name?' asked Biggles quickly.

'2472,' replied the other, with a queer smile.

'Mine's Bigglesworth—266 Squadron. Look me up sometime—goodbye.'

A swift handshake and Biggles was sprinting down the side of the hedge in the direction indicated by his preserver.

'Gosh! What jobs some people have to do. I wouldn't have that fellow's job for a million a year and a thousand V.C.s,' thought Biggles as, fifty yards down the hedge, he crawled through a convenient gap.

As he sprang erect the mist rolled away as if a giant curtain had been drawn, and the sun poured down in all its autumnal glory. There, ten yards away, stood the Camel, and beside it two German soldiers. They carried mess tins, and were evidently two of the party he had seen a few moments before.

With a bound, almost without pausing to think, Biggles was on them. The Germans swung round in alarm as they heard his swift approach, but Biggles held all the advantages of surprise attack. The first went down like a log before he had time to put his hands up as his jaw stopped a mighty swing from Biggles' right; the iron mess-tin rolled to one side as he fell. Biggles snatched it up by the strap and swung it with all his force straight at the head of the other German. It caught the man fairly and squarely on the temple and he dropped with a grunt like a pole-axed bullock. The whole thing was over almost before Biggles had realised the danger. With feverish speed he sprang to the cockpit of the Camel, switched on, turned the petrol on, and opened the throttle a fraction. Dashing back to the front of the machine he paused to feel the cylinders of the Bentley engine. They were not yet cold. He seized the propeller and whirled it with all his strength, almost falling backwards as it started with a roar. He tore madly round the wing and literally fell into the cockpit; once there, all his old confidence returned in a flash and

he looked eagerly around. Behind him the field
stretched open for a take-off; in the far corner some men
were running, pointing at him as they ran. He 'blipped'
the engine with the rudder hard over, almost swinging
the Camel round on its own axis, and for the first time
since he realized he was in enemy country he breathed
freely. He pushed the throttle open and tore across the
field like a blunt-nosed bullet; a moment later he was in
the air heading for the line, with the landscape lying
clear and plain below him.

A stab of orange flame and a cloud of black smoke
blossomed out in front of him, another, and another,
and Biggles twisted like a snipe to throw the archie
gunners off their mark. Strings of 'flaming onions' shot
past him and the sky was torn with fire and hurtling
metal.

'They're taking good care no one comes prowling
about here for long,' he observed, as he kicked out first
one foot and then the other to maintain his erratic
course in order to confuse the batteries below. He was
glad when the storm died down behind him. He surveyed the sky ahead intently. 'They saw me take off and
they'll phone every aerodrome between here and the
line to be on the look-out for me,' he told himself.

With his nose slightly down and engine at full throttle
he sped onwards. An aerodrome appeared ahead; he
could see little ant-like figures running around the
black-crossed machines which stood on the tarmac.
Something struck the Camel with a vibrating *sprang-g-g*,
and he knew the machine-gunners were busy. He put
his nose down in a fury and swept across the hangars
with his guns spurting a double stream of tracer, and
laughed as he saw the figures below sprinting for cover.
He zoomed up and roared on without waiting to see
what damage he had done.

A Fokker triplane, looking like a Venetian blind,

flashed down on his flank and the sight sent him fighting mad. The Camel made the lightning right-hand
turn for which it was famous and the twin Vickers guns
on the cowling poured a stream of bullets through the
Fokker's centre section. The Boche machine lurched
drunkenly and plunged down out of sight below.
Biggles continued his way without another glance. Far
away to his left he could see a formation of straight-
winged machines heading towards him, and he swept
still lower, literally hopping the trees and hedges that
stood in his path. The pock-marked desolation of the
trenches appeared below and Biggles thrilled at the
sight; he shot across them at fifty feet, wondering
vaguely where all the bullets that were being fired at
him were going.

He was over his own side of the lines now, and he
sagged lower in the cockpit with relief as he passed the
balloon line. Ten minutes later he landed at Maranique. Major Mullen was standing on the tarmac and
came to meet him as he taxied in.

'You've got back, then, Biggles—had a good leave?'

'Fine, sir, thanks,' responded Biggles.

'It's been pretty thick here. What time did you leave
this morning?'

'Oh, about sixish.'

'Then you must have called somewhere on the way—
I hope they gave you a good time?'

'They did that,' grinned Biggles as he climbed out of
the cockpit.

Major Mullen eyed his mud-plastered boots and coat
with astonishment. 'Good Lord!' he cried. 'Where the
deuce have you been?'

'On leave, sir,' smiled Biggles innocently. 'But I've
got an urgent message for H.Q.'

In a few words he described his adventures of the
morning, and ten minutes later his written report was

on its way by hand to Headquarters. One thing only he omitted—his finding of the gas plant. He reported its position, but the credit for that discovery he left to '2742'.

'That's the least I can do for him,' decided Biggles.

AFFAIRE DE CŒUR

BIGGLES hummed cheerfully as he cruised along in the new Camel which he had just fetched from the Aircraft Park.

'Another five minutes and I shall be home,' he thought, but fate willed otherwise. The engine coughed, coughed again, and, with a final splutter, expired, leaving him with a 'dead' prop. He exclaimed softly, pushed the joystick forward, and looked quickly around for the most suitable field for the now inevitable forced landing.

To the right lay the forest of Clarmes. 'Nothing doing that way,' he muttered, and looked down between his left wings. Ah! there it was. Almost on the edge of the forest was a large pasture, free from obstruction. The pilot, with a confidence born of long experience, side-slipped towards it, levelled out over the hedge and made a perfect three-point landing.

He sat in the cockpit for a minute or two contemplating his position; then he yawned, pushed up his goggles and prepared to take stock of his immediate surroundings. He raised his eyebrows appreciatively as he noted the sylvan beauty of the scene around him. Above, the sun shone from a cloudless blue sky. Straight before him a low lichen-covered stone wall enclosed an orchard through which he could just perceive a dull red pantiled roof. To the right lay the forest, cool and inviting. To the left a stream meandered smoothly between a double row of willows.

'Who said there was a war on?' he murmured, lighting a cigarette, and climbing up on to the 'hump' of his Camel, the better to survey the enchanting scene. 'Well,

well, let's see if anyone is at home.'

He sprang lightly to the ground, threw his leather coat across the fuselage, and strolled towards the house. An old iron gate opened into the orchard; entering, he paused for a moment, uncertain of the path.

'Are you looking for me, monsieur?' said a musical voice.

Turning, he beheld a vision of blonde loveliness, wrapped up in blue silk, smiling at him. For a moment he stared as if he had never seen a woman before. He closed his eyes, shook his head, and opened them again. The vision was still there, dimpling.

'You were looking for me, perhaps?' said the girl again.

Biggles saluted like a man sleep-walking.

'Mademoiselle,' he said earnestly, 'I've been looking for you all my life. I didn't think I'd ever find you.'

'Then why did you land here?' asked the girl.

'I landed here because my mag. shorted,' explained Biggles.

'What would have happened if you had not landed when your bag shorted?' inquired the vision curiously.

'Not bag—mag. Short for magneto, you know,' replied Biggles, grinning. 'Do you know, I've never even thought of doing anything but land when a mag. shorts; if I didn't, I expect that I should fall from a great altitude and collide with something substantial.'

'What are you going to do now?'

'I don't know—it takes thinking about. It may be necessary for me to stay here for some time. Anyway, the war will still be on when I get back. But, pardon me, mademoiselle, if I appear impertinent; are you English? I ask because you speak English so well.'

'Not quite, monsieur. My mother was English and I have been to school in England,' replied the girl.

'Thank you, Miss—er————'

'Marie Janis is my name.'

'A charming name more charming even than this spot of heaven,' said Biggles warmly. 'Have you a telephone, Miss Janis? You see, although the matter is not urgent, if I do not ring up my Squadron to say where I am someone may fly around to look for me,' he explained.

The thought of Mahoney spotting his Camel from the air and landing did not, in the circumstances, fill him with the enthusiasm one might normally expect.

'Come and use the telephone, M'sieur le Capitaine,' said the girl, leading the way. 'May I offer you *un petit verre?*'

'May you?' responded Biggles, warmly. 'I should say you may!'

Five hours later Biggles again took his place in the cockpit of the Camel, which a party of ack-emmas had now repaired. He took off and swung low over the orchard, waving gaily to a slim blue-clad figure that looked upwards and waved back.

Rosy clouds drifted across the horizon as he made the short flight back to the aerodrome.

'That girl's what I've been reading about,' he told himself. 'She's the "Spirit of the Air", and she's going to like me an awful lot if I know anything about it. Anyway, I'd be the sort of skunk who'd give rat poison to orphans if I didn't go back and thank her for her hospitality.'

Biggles, a week later, seated on an old stone bench in the orchard, sighed contentedly. The distant flickering beam of a searchlight on the war-stricken sky meant nothing to him; a little head, shining whitely in the moonlight, nestled lightly on his sleeve. In the short time that had elapsed since his forced landing he had made considerable progress.

'Tell me, Marie,' he said. 'Do you ever hear from your father?'

'No, m'sieur,' replied the girl sadly. 'I told you he was on a visit to the north when war was declared. In the wild panic of the Boche advance he was left behind in what is now the occupied territory. Communication with that part of France is forbidden, but I have had two letters from him which were sent by way of England by friends. I have not been able to tell him that mama is—dead!'

Tears shone for a moment in her eyes, and Biggles stirred uncomfortably.

'It is a hell of a war,' he said compassionately.

'If only I could get a letter to him to say that mama is dead and that I am looking after things until he returns I should be happy. Poor Papa!'

'I suppose you don't even know where he is?' said Biggles sympathetically.

'But yes,' answered the girl quickly; 'I know where he is. He is still at our friend's chateau, where he was staying when the Boche came in.'

'Where's that?' asked Biggles in surprise.

'At Vinard, near Lille; le Chateau Borceau,' she replied. 'But he might as well be in Berlin,' she concluded sadly, shrugging her shoulders.

'Good Lord!' ejaculated Biggles suddenly.

'Why did you say that, monsieur?'

'Nothing—only an idea struck me, that's all,' said Biggles.

'Tell me.'

'No. I'm crazy. Better forget it.'

'Tell me—please.'

Biggles wavered. 'All right,' he said. 'Say "please, Biggles," and I'll tell you.'

'Please, Beegles.'

Biggles smiled at the pronunciation. 'Well, if you

must know,' he said, 'it struck me that I might act as a messenger for you.'

'Beegles! How?'

'I had some crazy notion that I might be able to drop a letter from my machine,' explained Biggles.

'*Mon dieu!*' The girl sprang to her feet in excitement, but Biggles held her arm and pulled her towards him.

For a moment she resisted, and then slipped into his arms. 'Beegles—please.'

'Marie,' whispered Biggles, as their lips met. Then, his heart beating faster than archie or enemy aircraft had ever caused it to beat, he suddenly pushed her aside, rose to his feet and looked at the luminous dial of his watch. 'Time I was getting back to quarters,' he said unsteadily.

'But, Beegles, it is not yet so late.'

Biggles sat down, passed his hand over his face, and then laughed. 'My own mag. was nearly shorting then,' he said.

They both laughed, and the spell was broken.

'Tell me, Beegles, is it possible to drop such a letter to Papa?' said the girl presently.

'I don't know,' said Biggles, a trifle anxiously. 'I don't know what orders are about that sort of thing, and that's a fact. There wouldn't be any harm in it, and they wouldn't know about, it, anyway. You give me the letter and I'll see what I can do.'

'Beegles—you————'

'Well?'

'Never mind. Come to the house and we will write the letter together.'

Hand in hand they walked slowly towards the house. The girl took a writing-pad from a desk and began to write; the door opened noiselessly and Antoine, Marie's elderly manservant, appeared.

'Did you ring, mademoiselle?' he asked.

'Merci, Antoine.'

'Do you know,' said Biggles, after the man had withdrawn, 'I don't like the look of that bloke. I never saw a nastier-looking piece of work in my life.'

'But what should I do without Antoine, and Lucille, his wife? They are the only two that stayed with me all the time. Antoine is a dear; he thinks only of me,' said the girl reproachfully.

'I see,' said Biggles. 'Well, go ahead with the letter.'

The girl wrote rapidly.

'Look,' she smiled when it was finished. 'Read it and tell me if you do not think it is a lovely letter to a long-lost father.'

Biggles read the first few lines and skipped the rest, blushing. 'I don't want to read your letter, kid,' he said.

Marie sealed the letter, addressed it, and tied it firmly to a small paperweight. 'Now,' she said; 'what can we use for a banner?'

'You mean a streamer,' laughed Biggles.

'Yes, a streamer. Why! Here is the very thing.' She took a black-and-white silk scarf from the back of a chair and tied the paper-weight to it. 'There you are, *mon aviateur*,' she laughed. 'Take care; do not hit Papa on the head or he will wish I had not written.'

Biggles slipped the packet into the pocket of his British 'warm' and took her in his arms impatiently.

Arriving at the aerodrome he went to his quarters and flung the coat on the bed, and then made his way across to the mess for a drink. As the door of his quarters closed behind him, two men—an officer in uniform and a civilian—entered the room. Without a moment's hesitation the civilian picked up the coat and removed the letter from the pocket.

'You know what to do,' he said grimly.

'How long will you be?'

'An hour. Not more. Keep him until 11.30, to be on

the safe side,' said the civilian.

'I will,' replied the officer, and followed Biggles into the mess.

Biggles, humming gaily, headed for home. His trip had proved uneventful and the dropping of Marie's letter ridiculously simple. He had found the chateau easily, and swooping low had seen the black-and-white scarf flutter on to the lawn. Safely back across the line he was now congratulating himself upon the success of his mission. S.287, the neighbouring S.E.5 Squadron, lay below, and it occurred to him to land and pass the time of day with them.

Conscious that many eyes would be watching him, he side-slipped in and flattened out for his most artistic landing. There was a sudden crash, the Camel swung violently and tipped up on to its nose. Muttering savagely, he climbed out and surveyed the damage.

'Why the deuce don't you f-llows put a flag or something on this sunken road?' he said bitterly to Wilkinson and other pilots who had hurried to the scene; he pointed to the cause of his misadventure. 'Look at that mess.'

'Well, most people know about that road,' said Wilkinson. 'If I'd have known you were coming I'd have had it filled in altogether. Never mind; it's only a tyre and the prop. gone. Our fellows will have it right by tomorrow. Come and have a drink; I'll find you transport to take you home. The C.O.'s on leave, so you can use his car.'

'Righto, but I'm not staying to dinner,' said Biggles emphatically. 'I'm on duty tonight,' he added, thinking of a moonlit orchard and an old stone seat.

It was nearly eight o'clock when he left the aerodrome, seated at the wheel of the borrowed car. He had rung up Major Mullen and told him that he would be late, and now, thrilling with anticipation, he headed for the home of the girl who was making his life worth living and the war worth fighting for.

The night was dark, for low clouds were drifting across the face of the moon; a row of distant archie-bursts made him look up, frowning. A bomb raid, inter-rupting the story of his successful trip, was the last thing he wanted. His frown deepened as the enemy aircraft and the accompanying archie drew nearer.

'They're coming right over the house, confound 'em,' he said, and switching off his lights raced for the orchard. 'My gosh, they're low!' he muttered, as he tore down the road, the roar of the engines of the heavy bombers in his ears. 'They're following this road, too.' He wondered where they were making for, trying to recall any possible objective on their line of flight. That he himself might be in danger did not even occur to him. He was less than five miles from the house now and taking desperate chances to race the machines. 'The poor kid'll be scared stiff if they pass over her as low as this.'

With every nerve taut he tore down the road. He caught his breath suddenly. What was that? A whist-ling screech filled his ears and an icy hand clutched his heart. Too well he knew the sound. *Boom! Boom! Boom!* Three vivid flashes of orange fire leapt towards the sky. *Boom! Boom! Boom!*—and then three more.

'What are they fanning, the fools? There is only the forest there,' thought Biggles, as, numb with shock, he raced round the last bend. Six more thundering detona-tions, seemingly a hundred yards ahead, nearly split his eardrums, but still he did not pause. He tried to think, but could not; he had lost all sense of time and reason. He seemed to have been driving for ever, and he mut-tered as he drove. Searchlights probed the sky on all sides and subconsciously he noticed that the noise of the engines was fading into the distance.

'They're gone,' he said, trying hard to think clearly. 'What if they've hit the house?'

He jammed on his brakes with a grinding screech as two men sprang out in front of the car as he turned in the gates; but he was not looking at them. One glance showed him that the house was a blazing pile of ruins. He sprang out of the car and darted towards the conflagration, but a hand closed on his arm like a vice.

Biggles, white-faced, turned and struck out viciously. 'My girl's in there,' he muttered.

A sharp military voice penetrated his stunned brain. 'Stand fast, Captain Bigglesworth,' it said.

'Let me go,' snarled Biggles, struggling like a madman.

'One more word from you, Captain Bigglesworth, and I'll put you under arrest,' said the voice harshly.

'You'll what?' Biggles turned, his brain fighting for consciousness. 'You'll what?' he cried again incredulously.

He saw the firelight gleam on the fixed bayonets of a squad of Tommies; Colonel Raymond of Wing Headquarters and another man stood near them. Biggles passed his hand over his eyes, swaying.

'I'm dreaming,' he said; 'that's it, dreaming. What a nightmare! I wish I could wake up.'

'Take a drink, Bigglesworth, and pull yourself together,' said Colonel Raymond, passing him a flask.

Biggles emptied the flask and handed it back.

'I'm going now,' said the Colonel. 'I'll see you in the morning. This officer will tell you all you need to know,' he concluded, indicating a dark-clad civilian standing near. 'Good night, Bigglesworth.'

'Good night, sir.'

'Tell me,' said Biggles, with an effort, 'is she—in there?'

The man nodded.

'Then that's all I need to know,' said Biggles, slowly turning away.

'I'm sorry, but there are other things you will have to know,' returned the man.

'Who are you?' said Biggles curiously.

'Major Charles, of the British Intelligence Service.'

'Intelligence!' repeated Biggles, the first ray of light bursting upon him.

'Come here a moment.' Major Charles switched on the light of his car. 'Yesterday, a lady asked you to deliver a message for her, did she not?' he asked.

'Why—yes.'

'Did you see it?'

'Yes!'

'Was this it?' said Major Charles, handing him a letter.

Biggles read the first few lines, dazed. 'Yes,' he said; 'that was it.'

'Turn it over.'

Unconsciously Biggles obeyed. He started as his eyes fell on a tangle of fine lines that showed up clearly. In the centre was a circle.

'Do you recognise that?'

'Yes.'

'What is it.'

'It is a map of 266 Squadron aerodrome,' replied Biggles, like a child reciting a catechism.

'You see the circle?'

'Yes.'

'The Officers' Mess. Perhaps you understand now. The letter you were asked to carry had been previously prepared with a solution of invisible ink and contained such information that, had you delivered it, your entire squadron would have been wiped out tonight, and you as well. The girl sent you to your death, Captain Bigglesworth.'

'I'll not believe it,' said Biggles distinctly. 'But I did deliver the letter, anyway,' he cried suddenly.

'Not this one,' said Major Charles, smiling queerly. 'You delivered the one we substituted.'

'Substituted?'

'We have watched this lady for a long time. You have been under surveillance since the day you force-landed, although your record put you above suspicion.'

'And on the substituted plan you marked her home to be bombed instead of the aerodrome?' sneered Biggles. 'Why?'

Major Charles shrugged his shoulders. 'The lady was well connected. There may have been unexpected difficulties connected with an arrest, yet her activities had to be checked. She had powerful friends in high places. Well, I must be going; no doubt you will hear from Wing in the morning.'

Biggles walked a little way up the garden path. The old stone seat glowed dully crimson. 'Bah!' he muttered, turning. 'What a fool I am. What a hell of a war this is.'

He drove slowly back to the aerodrome. On his table lay a letter. Ripping it open eagerly, he said:

Darling,

I have something important to ask you— something you must do for me. Tonight at seven o'clock I will come for you. It is important. Meet me in the road by the aerodrome. I will be very kind to you, my Biggles.

MARIE.

Biggles, with trembling hands, sat on the bed and re-read the letter, trying to reason out its purpose. 'She timed the raid for eight,' he said to himself, 'when all officers would be dining in the mess. She knew I should be there and wrote this to bring me out. She knew I'd never leave her waiting on the road—that was the way of it. She must have cared, or she wouldn't have done that. When I didn't come she went back home. She didn't know I hadn't seen her letter—how could she? Now she's dead. If I hadn't landed at 287 I should be with her now. Well, she'll never know.'

He rose wearily. Voices were singing in the distance, and he smiled bitterly as he heard the well-remembered words:

> Who minds to the dust returning.
>> Who shrinks from the sable shore,
> Where the high and haughty yearning
>> Of the soul shall be no more?

> So stand by your glasses steady,
>> This world is a world of lies;
> A cup to the dead already,
>> Hurrah! for the next man who dies.

A knock at the door aroused him from his reverie. An orderly of the guard entered.

'A lady left this for you,' he said, holding out a letter.

'A lady—when?' said Biggles, holding himself in hand with a mighty effort.

'About ten minutes ago, sir. Just before you came in. She came about eight and said she must see you, sir, but I told her you weren't here.'

'Where is she now?'

'She's gone, sir; she was in a car. She told me to bring the letter straight to you when you returned, sir.'

'All right—you may go.'

Biggles took the letter, fighting back a wild desire to shout, opened it, and read:

Goodbye, my Biggles.

You know now. What can I say? Only this. Our destinies are not always in our own hands—always try and remember that, my Biggles. That is all I may say. I came tonight to take you away or die with you, but you were not here. And remember that one thing in this world of war and lies is true; my love for you. It may help, as it helps me. Take care of yourself. Always I shall pray for you. If anything happens to you I shall know, but if to me you will never know. My last thought will be of you. We shall meet again, if not in this world then in the next, so I will not say goodbye.

Au revoir,
MARIE.

'And they think she's dead,' said Biggles softly. 'She risked her life to tell me this.'

He kissed the letter tenderly, then held it to the candle and watched it burn away.

He was crumbling the ashes between his fingers when the door opened, and Mahoney entered. 'Hullo, laddie, what's wrong; had a fire?' he enquired.

'Yes,' replied Biggles slowly; 'foolish of me; got my fingers burnt a bit, too.'

THE LAST SHOW

IN the days that followed the tragic *affaire*, Biggles flew with abandon and with such an utter disregard of consequences that Major Mullen knew that if he persisted it could only be a matter of time before he 'failed to return'. The C.O. had not mentioned the affair of the girl to him, but Biggles knew that he must be aware of the main facts of the case, or he would certainly have asked him why he had been called to Headquarters.

However much the Major knew he said nothing, but he watched his flight-commander's behaviour with deep-rooted anxiety. He called MacLaren and Mahoney into his office to discuss the matter with them.

Mahoney nodded sympathetically as he listened to the C.O.'s plaint. 'Biggles is finished unless he takes a rest', he said. 'He's drinking, and you know what that means—he's going fast. Of course, a fellow doesn't get drunk when he's in the state Biggles is in. It's no use talking to him—you know that as well as I do. He's got to the stage when he takes advice as a personal affront against his flying. It's a pity, but most of us go that way at the end, I suppose. Newland, of 287, told me confidentially the other day that a blue pigeon follows him in the air wherever he goes, and he meant it.'

'Well, I shall have to send him home, whether he likes it or not,' went on the Major, 'but it will break his heart if I don't find a good excuse. Now look, you fellows. I've got to send somebody home to form a new Squadron—of Snipes, I believe—and bring it over. You are both senior to Bigglesworth; you are both due for promotion. I shall be going to Wing in a week or two,

I hear, so one of you will have to take over 266. Do
you mind if I send Bigglesworth home for the new
Squadron?' The C.O. looked at the two captains
apologetically.

'Not me, sir,' said Mahoney instantly.

'Nor I, sir,' echoed MacLaren.

'Thank you. That's what I wanted to know,' said the
Major. 'I'll send him home, then. Where is he now?'

'He's in the air,' replied Mahoney. 'He's never on the
ground. Goodness knows where he goes; it must be
miles over; I never see him on patrol.'

The C.O. nodded. 'Well, he can't get away with that
much longer. They're bound to get him. By the way,
there's a big show tomorrow—it will be in orders
tonight. You'd better have a good look round your
machines.'

Biggles, cruising at 18,000 feet, turned in the direction of Lille without being really conscious of the fact.
He surveyed the surrounding air coldly and dispassionately for signs of enemy aircraft, but except for a
formation of Bristol Fighters homeward bound, far
below, the sky was empty. His thoughts wandered back
to the girl who had come into his life. Where was she
now? Where had she gone on that tragic night of dis-
illusionment? Had she been caught? That was the
thought that made the day a torture and the night a
horror. He visualized her in the cold-grey of dawn with
a bandage over her eyes facing a firing party in some
gloomy French prison.

A volley of shots rang out, something jerked the
rudder-bar from his feet and brought him back to the
realities of life with a start.

He half-rolled and looked around; a Hannoverian
was rapidly receding into the distance. He frowned at it
in surprise and consternation. 'Good Lord! I must have

nearly flown into it without seeing it, and the observer had a crack at me as he went by,' he mused. 'If it had been a D.VII———' He shrugged his shoulders. What did it matter—what did anything matter?

He looked downwards to pick up his bearings; the landscape was familar, for he had seen it a dozen times during the past week. To the left lay Lille, the worst hot-bed of archie in the whole of France. On his right a narrow, winding road led to the village of Vinard and the Chateau Boreau—his only link with Marie. She might even be there now—the thought occurred to him for the first time. How could she have reached it? Spies went to and fro across the line, he reflected; nobody knew how, except the chosen few whose hazardous business it was. He looked around the sky, but could see nothing; he put the stick forward and commenced to spiral down in wide circles.

At 5,000 feet he hesitated. Dare he risk losing any more height? He looped, half-rolled, came out and looped again, half-rolling off the top of it. Then he spun. He came out at 2,000 feet and studied the chateau intently. No one was in sight—yes—his eye caught a movement at the end of the garden and he glided lower. He knew that he was taking a foolish risk, but his curiosity overcame his caution.

Someone was waving—what? He put his nose down in a swift dive and then zoomed upwards exultantly, his heart beating tumultuously. Had his eyes betrayed him or had he seen a blue-clad figure waving a blue-and-white scarf? He looked back; the blue-and-white scarf was spread on the lawn. He turned the Camel in the direction of the line and raced for home, his mind in a whirl.

'I'm mad,' he grated between his clenched teeth. 'She must be a spy or she wouldn't be there.' The thought seemed to chill him, and only then did he realize that he still hoped that the authorities were mistaken in their belief that she was engaged in espionage.

Doubts began to assail him. Had he really seen her— or had it been a trick of the imagination? It might have been someone else; he was too far away to recognize features.

'She's a spy anyway. I must be stark, staring mad,' he told himself, as he dodged and twisted away from a close salvo of archie.

Half-way home he had the good fortune to fall in with a formation of S.E.5s, to which he attached himself. Safely over the lines he waved them farewell and was soon back at Maranique. He made his way to the mess and thrust himself into a group of officers clustered around the noticeboard.

'What's on, chaps?' he asked.

'Big show tomorrow, Biggles ' replied Mahoney.

'What is it?'

'Escort—a double dose. Eighteen "Nines" are bombing Aerodrome 27 in the morning and the same lot are doing an objective near Lille in the afternoon. We and 287 are escorting. 287 are up in the gallery, and we're sticking with the formation. Rendezvous over Mossy-face at 10,000 feet at ten ack-emma.'

'Great Scott! Have they discovered the German Headquarters Staff or something?'

'Shouldn't be surprised. Must be something important to do the shows. The Aerodrome 27 show was on first—and the second show came through later. They must be going to try and blot something off the map; the idea's all right if the bombers could only hit the thing.'

Biggles nodded moodily, for the show left him unmoved. Escort was a boring business, particularly in his present state of mind. Later in the evening another notice was put on the board, which was greeted with loud cheers. Biggles forced his way to the front rank of the group and read:

Promotions
Act. Cpt. J. Bigglesworth, M.C., to Major, W.E.F. 10.11.18 (Authority) P.243/117/18.

Postings
Major J. Bigglesworth, from 266 Squadron to Command 319 Squadron. H.E., W.E.F. 11.11.18. P.243/118/18.

Biggles looked at the notice unbelievingly. He turned to Major Mullen, who had just entered.

'So I'm going home, sir,' he said in a strained voice.

'Yes, Bigglesworth. Wing wants you to fetch 319 out. I believe you're getting Snipes—you'll be able to make rings round Camels.

'Camels are good enough for me,' protested Biggles. 'That's the trouble with this infernal war. People are never satisfied. Let us stick to Camels and S.E.s and let the Boche have their D. Sevens, instead of all this chopping and changing about. I've heard a rumour about a new kite called a Salamander that carries a sheet of armour plate. Why? I'll tell you. Some brasshat's got hit in the pants and that's the result. What with sheet iron, oxygen to blow your inside out, and electrically heated clothing to set fire to your kidneys, this war is going to bits.'

'You'll talk differently when you get your Snipes,' laughed the Major.

'Orders say I'm to move off tomorrow.'

'Yes, that's right.'

'Good. You can give my love to the Huns at Aerodrome 27 and—what's the name of the other target they're going to fan down?'

'Oh, it's a new one to me,' replied the Major. 'Place

near Lille—Chateau Boreau or something like that—
cheerio—see you later.'

It was as well that he did not pause to take a second
glance at his flight-commander's face, or he might have
asked awkward questions. For a full minute Biggles
remained rooted to the spot with the words ringing in
his ears.

'Chateau Boreau, eh?' he said, under his breath. 'So
they know about that. How the deuce did those nosy-
parkers on Intelligence find that out?' he muttered
bitterly.

Mahoney slapped him on the back. 'Have a drink,
Biggles?' he cried.

Biggles swung round. 'Go to—— No, I didn't
mean that, old lad,' he said quickly. 'I was a bit upset at
leaving the Squadron. Sorry—what are you having,
everybody?' he called aloud. 'Drinks are on me tonight.'

Dinner was a boisterous affair; the usual farewell
speeches were made and everybody was noisily happy.
Biggles, pale-faced, with his eyes gleaming unnaturally,
held the board.

'So tomorrow I am doing my last show,' he concluded.

The C.O. looked up quickly. 'But I thought you were
going in the morning,' he exclaimed in surprise.

'In the afternoon, if you don't mind, sir,' answered
Biggles. 'I must do one more show with 266.'

Major Mullen nodded. 'All right,' he said; 'but don't
take any chances,' he added. 'I ought to pack you off in
the morning really.'

Biggles spent a troubled and restless night. Why he
had asked to be allowed to fly with the morning show he
hardly knew, unless it was to delay departure as long as
possible. He racked his brain to find an excuse to post-
pone it until the evening in order to learn the result of
the bombing of the Chateau. If he was unable to do

that, he had decided to ask Mac or Mahoney to try to send him copies of the photographs of the bomb-bursts.

Thinking things over, he realised that his first fears that the Chateau was to be bombed because Intelligence had learned that Marie had made her way there were unfounded. It was far more likely that they had known for some time that the building housed certain members of the German Headquarters or Intelligence Staff, and the recent trouble had simply served to expedite their decision to bomb it.

What could he do about it? Nothing, he decided despairingly, absolutely nothing. It crossed his mind that he might drop a message of warning, but he dismissed the thought at once, because such an act would definitely make him a traitor to his own side. The thought of returning to England and leaving the girl to her fate without lifting a finger to save her nearly drove him to distraction. After all, the girl had tried to save him when the position had been reversed!

He was glad when his batman brought him early morning tea, and he arose, weary and hollow-eyed. Ten o'clock found him in the air heading for the line and the Boche aerodrome at Lille. Behind him were Cowley and Algernon Montgomery. On his left were the bombers, the sun flashing on their varnished wings, the observers leaning carelessly on their Scarff rings. Beyond was Mahoney and 'A' Flight. Somewhere in the rear was Maclaren and 'B' Flight, while two thousand feet about he could see the S.E.5s.

'What a sight,' thought Biggles, as his eyes swept over the thirty-six machines; 'it will take a Hun with some nerve to tackle this lot.'

The observer in the nearest 'Nine' waved him, crossed his fingers and pointed. Biggles, following the direction indicated, saw half-a-dozen Fokker Triplanes flying parallel with them. Presently they turned away

and disappeared into the distance. The observer waved
and laughed and held out his hands with the thumbs
turned up.

'Yes,' agreed Biggles mentally; 'they spotted the
S.E.s up top. They've thought better of it, and I don't
wonder.'

He was sorry that the Huns had departed, for he was
aching for action. For three-quarters of an hour they
flew steadily into enemy sky, and then the leader of the
bombers, conspicuous by his streamers, began to turn.

'He's coming round into the wind,' thought Biggles.
'We must be over the objective.'

He looked down and beheld the aerodrome. He
looked up again just in time to see the leader fire a green
Very light. Eighteen 112-lb. bombs swung off their
racks into space.

A moment later a second lot of eighteen bombs followed the first. Keeping a watchful eye on his position
in the formation Biggles snatched quick glances at the
earth below. What a time it seemed to take the bombs to
reach the ground.

'Dash it, they can't all be duds,' he muttered. 'Ah,
there they go!'

A group of smoke-bursts appeared on the aerodrome,
and, a moment later, another group.

The second lot were better than the first. One bomb
had fallen directly on to a hangar, one had burst among
the machines on the tarmac, and another had struck
some buildings just behind. The rest of the bombs had
scattered themselves over the aerodrome.

'There will have to be a lot of spade work there before
anybody will try any night-landings,' grinned Biggles,
as he visualised the havoc the bombs had caused to the
surface of the aerodrome.

The faint crackle of guns reached his ears above the

noise of the engines; he looked quickly over his shoulder and caught his breath as his eyes fell on a mixed swarm of Fokker D.VIIs and Triplanes coming down almost vertically on the rearmost 'Nines'. The gunners in the back seats were crouching low behind their Lewis guns. For a brief moment, as the enemy came within range, the air was full of sparkling lines of tracer, and then the Fokkers disappeared through and below the bombers.

He saw MacLaren's machine wallow for a moment like a rolling porpoise, and then, with the rest of his Flight, plunge down in the wake of the enemy machines.

'Suffering heavens! There must be thirty of them, and they mean business, coming in like that,' thought Biggles, as he rocked his wings and roared down into the whirling medley below. A red-painted machine crossed his sights and he pressed his triggers, but had to jerk round in a steep bank to avoid colliding with the first of the S.E.s which were coming down from above. He glanced around swiftly. The air about him was full of machines, diving, zooming and circling; the bombers had held on their course and were already a mile away.

He flung his Camel on the tail of a blue-and-white Fokker, and the same instant there was a splintering jar as something crashed through his instrument board. A burning pain paralysed his leg, and he twisted desperately to try to see his opponent. Huns were all round him shooting his machine to pieces. He pulled the joy-stick back into his stomach and zoomed wildly. A Fokker flashed into his sights; he saw his tracer pour straight through it; the pilot slumped forward in his seat and the nose of the machine went down in an engine stall as the withering blast of lead struck it.

Something lashed the Camel like a cat-o'-nine-tails; he felt the machine quiver, and the next moment he was spinning, fighting furiously to get the machine on an even keel. A feeling of nauseating helplessness swept over him as he realized that the Camel was not answering to the controls.

Something strange seemed to be whirling on the end of his wing-tip, and he saw it was an aileron, hanging by a single wire. He kicked on the opposite rudder and the nose of the Camel came up.

'If I can only keep her there,' was the thought that flashed through his brain; but another burst of fire from an unseen foe tore through his centre section and he instinctively kicked out his right foot. The Camel spun again at once. He was near the ground now and he fought to get the nose of the machine up again, but something seemed to have gone wrong with his leg. He couldn't move it.

Biggles knew his time had come. He knew he was going down under a hail of lead in just the same way as he had seen dozens of machines going down, as he himself had sent them down. He knew he was going to crash, but the knowledge left 'im unmoved. A thousand thoughts crowded into his mind in a second of time that seemed like minutes; in that brief moment he thought of a dozen things he might do as the machine struck.

The nose of the Camel half came up—slowly—and the machine stopped spinning.

The Camel was side-slipping steeply to the right now, nose down, on the very verge of another spin that would be the last. The joystick was back in his left thigh and he unfastened his belt and twisted in his seat to get his right foot on the left side of the rudder, but it had no effect. A row of poplars appeared to leap upwards to meet him; he switched off the ignition with a lightning sweep of his hand, lifted the knee of his unwounded leg to his chin, folded his arms across his face and awaited the impact.

There was a splintering, rending crash, like a great

tree in a forest falling on undergrowth. With the horror of fire upon him he clawed his way frantically out of the tangled wreck and half-rolled and half-crawled away from it. He seemed to be moving in a ghastly nightmare from which he could not awake. He became vaguely aware of the heat of a conflagration near him; it was the Camel, blazing furiously. Strange-looking soldiers were running towards him and he tore off his blood-stained goggles and stared at them, trying to grasp what had happened and what was happening.

'I'm down,' he muttered to himself in a voice which he hardly recognised as his own. 'I'm down,' he said again, as if the sound of the words would help him to understand.

The German soldiers were standing in a circle around him now, and he looked at them curiously. One of them stepped forward. '*Schweinhund flieger!*' he grunted, and kicked him viciously in the side.

Biggles bit his lip at the pain. The man raised his heavy boot again, but there was a sudden authoritative word of command and he stepped back hastily. Biggles looked up to see and officer of about his own age, in a tight-fitting pale-grey uniform, regarding him compassionately. He noted the Pour-le-Merite Order at his throat, and the Iron Cross of the First Class below.

'So you have had bad luck,' he said, in English, with scarcely a trace of accent.

'Yes,' replied Biggles with an effort, forcing a smile and trying to get on his feet. 'And I am sorry it happened this morning.'

'Why?'

'Because I particularly wanted to see a raid this afternoon,' he answered.

'Yes? But there will be no raid this afternoon,' replied the German, smiling.

'Why not?'

The German laughed softly. 'An armistice was signed half an hour ago—but, of course, you didn't know.'

There are many other exciting Biggles books published in Armada.

Here are some of them:

BIGGLES LEARNS TO FLY

The story of how Biggles, at seventeen, joined the Royal Flying Corps and after only fifteen hours of solo-flying went to war.

BIGGLES IN THE BALTIC

Biggles takes a secret squadron to a rocky island in the Baltic. Their deadly mission—to harry the Germans behind enemy lines.

BIGGLES HITS THE TRAIL

A sinister group in the mysterious land of Tibet plan to conquer the world—Biggles, Algy and Ginger help to foil them.

BIGGLES IN THE ORIENT

Hair-raising danger awaits Biggles in the jungles of Asia, when he is called in to solve the mystery of a deadly Japanese secret weapon.

BIGGLES FOLLOWS ON

When British soldiers start deserting, Biggles finds himself hot on the trail of his arch-enemy, Von Stalhein— a trail that ends in a desperate raid on a secret military base on the far side of the world.

Armada